A
Twisted Shade
OF
Green

PORTRAYAL OF LUST
AND REVENGE

ELOISE EPPS MACKINNON

authorHOUSE®

AuthorHouse™
1663 Liberty Drive
Bloomington, IN 47403
www.authorhouse.com
Phone: 1 (800) 839-8640

Published by AuthorHouse 07/09/2018

ISBN: 978-1-5462-4996-2 (sc)
ISBN: 978-1-5462-4997-9 (e)

Library of Congress Control Number: 2018907997

Print information available on the last page.

Any people depicted in stock imagery provided by Getty Images are models, and such images are being used for illustrative purposes only. Certain stock imagery © Getty Images.

This book is printed on acid-free paper.

This Book is dedicated, first and foremost, to God. The Author and Finisher of it! And, my Mother, Trannie Rae Epps!

Secondly, I dedicate it to all of my loved ones; daughters, grandchildren, and sister, who went through the storm with me on the writing and editing of this novel.

Thank You, and I Love You All!!!

Prologue

June 15, 2012, Move-in day! A date Kali Mathias will remember for life. This was no ordinary day for Kali, as she packs up the last of her belongings while waiting on the movers to arrive. Kali was nearing forty years of life and has been dumped by more men than the law allows for one woman. But, today Kali's ecstatic to leave those men worries behind as she invites her sidekicks along; a few extra love handles and self-doubt uptown to mingle with the upper crest of society. She's going to rub noses with the Springfield, Virginia ballers; and her long-time, gossipy friend, Martha Hayward.

Not only was Kali entering into a strange world. She is moving her low self-esteem along with feelings of not being enough; pretty enough, skinny enough, or worthy enough. But oddly enough, she casts her lustful eyes on a man's soul that's held by another, and the desired one of every woman's palate in Springfield.

A fit man, who's 5'11" tall, dark, strapping physique shrieks sex appeal from the top of his head to the tip of his toes. A man, Kali didn't have the prettiness to allure but desired with every inch of her being. So many ladies desire to take a ride on Glen Monroe's arm. But did not understand what the going rate was for a Seasonal Man, nor his style of love, lust, deceit, and money it requires; other than his current seasonal; Jo-Ann Parks.

Nonetheless, it was the seasonal love sought-after by all of Springfield's finest; even Kali Mathias. But, unlike Jo-Ann Parks and all the rest, Kali has what most of the other women didn't. Kali has lots of money and a quick calculating mind to know beauty wasn't her undisclosed weapon. Kali uses what she has the most of to entice all men to take a second eyeful; money. The more cash she tempts a man's ego with, the more he thirsts Kali's love and affection. Some were able to flee Kali's web of cash bribes such as Joseph Carlson; however, she was certain it would be a welcoming invitation for Glen Monroe.

After what seems like a lifetime of being disregarded by Mr. Glen Monroe. Kali gets valorous! Kali decides if the man didn't want to come to her, then she'll take the party to him. As Kali confidently sashays into Hay-Way Market, Glen's workplace on a sunshiny, warm summer day. It has been almost two years since Kali moved into Springfield. Kali's day has finally come as she cruises up and down Glen's market aisles trying to gets a bit better acquainted with him. Kali begins to get a feel for him as a man; like she is exploring the heart of his very soul.

Kali knows she could trap Glen with one of his own demons; money. It's a scheme that Kali's been planning since the moment she moved to Springfield; even when Joseph Carlson ramshackle through the wall of her core stampeding upon her life. Kali smile as she utters. "One might even say, God has a sense of humor!" Mainly this man of Kali's dream always seems to come forth at that moment, she desires Glen Monroe the most. Somehow, momentarily snatching Kali's prize away from her mind for an earth-shattering, temporary fix. Only, placing her heart that much farther away from Glen's; the one man, Kali's body, craves him night-after-night.

Kali walks to Glen's register with the bribes in hand. She sees Glen's eyes hook in on the two-hundred dollar bottle of champagne, but Glen isn't basing Kali's worth on the two-hundred dollar bottle of champagne. Glen's greedy eyes were fixated on the payment with her Black American Express Card. In his head as the cha-ching of the cash register add up Kali's entrapment items, Glen's susceptible eyes were growing faithfully in-love with her Black American Express card. Smiling, he avidly voices. "Why hellooo beautiful! My name is Glen Monroe, and I'm the Store Manager here." He beams sinfully at Kali. "Did you find everything your heart was searching after or did you forget one thing in your cart?" Of course, he is referring to himself as the forgotten item on her list.

Batting her long sexy eyelashes, Kali teasingly laughs as she glances into Glen's eyes uttering. "You could not possibly be referring to yourself, as my missing object?"

Kali keeps on playfully trying to lead Glen on, as she returns his scandalous smile followed by a sexy wink.

Glaring nonstop into her face, he licks his lips a little before expelling. "Well, from the looks of your bag, it is a bit empty when I'm available in twenty minutes!"

From that moment on, Kali knows she has ensnared Glen's heart. However; it was Kali whose introduced to a new realism; a world which belongs to; no other, then Glen Monroe. A place where a woman discovers a taste of a scorned man's heartbreak, lust, and greed as a prize for his own justice. An area where Glen's colorful invite is only offered to ladies of wealth by personal invitation to enter. An empire of a Seasonal Man where there's no escape for your heart or soul, not unless Glen desires to set you free. An undisclosed land, where passion makes one believe she has Glen's entire world at their feet, but at the same time, she must lose her soul to have. A hold of sapid vengeance which quickly entraps Kali's essence camouflaged by love sugarcoated with deception, greed, and lust.

Chapter One

*K*ali Mathias sits in the kitchen near the double-glass patio door of her new home gazing out. Kali figures the move should have solved all her deceitful man issues, as she sits questioning herself. "Where did I go wrong?"

She just can't seem to sort out her life or understand why love has mistreated her so! Kali always thought she was invincible. The perfect large nine-bedroom colonial house on the lakefront, posh car, her own business, and good friends. But, most of all, Kali has this sizable bank account. It's that kind of bankroll where her money just seems to keep growing on a tree. Well, at least it is what her; so called, boyfriends consider to be true. For them, Kali has become the local ATM. When her friends look in Kali's face, their eyes only see a bright neon billboard in king-sized letters flashing "**BANK**" that spreads over her naïve forehead.

But now the lies, deception, and lustfulness of Kali's life is budding all over again. Kali heard thru the society rumormonger the latest saga about Mr. Joseph Carlson. Joseph was Kali's first lover since moving to Springfield and already caught tipping out on her with the girl next-door; Carol Benson. Who's suppose to be Kali's friend!

Hearing that news, Kali feels her life was over as she edges on the age of forty, and about to become manless at this same time. "How was it all possible?" Kali softly voices to herself while in tears.

She knew for sure Joseph was the one. Kali has been praying for a man to come into her life for so long. Kali was starting to believe God had forgotten to answer her lonesome prayer. When out of the blue, Joseph stepped into her life with a burst of sunshine. But, just as fast as Joseph stepped in, he left leaving Kali alone again. Now Kali felt cast aside by God as she sadly questions Him.

She states. "God, I believed Joseph was part of Your plans for me." She prays, "Lord, please show me where I went wrong? Besides, what's Carol got that I don't?"

Joseph's nomadic eyes were always a concern to Kali in the relationship. Though; quite a distasteful situation, Kali knew Joseph's passion for her was not solely based on love. Still, Kali's heart feels Joseph was that one man who kindles such a desire inside her; not only to trust in herself but to give love another chance. Perhaps, she's a bit baffled where these feelings were coming from. Was she basing it on the extra good loving she was receiving from him? Since Joseph has what it takes to make a bed go rocking in her wee hours of the night, and a treasure chest hunt for its pirate. Needless to say; Kali's losing it all, Joseph and all his thrills. Kali's little half-hearted life is suddenly reverting back to a manless existence. It was shattering her happy world into tiny pieces to know she had lost Joseph. But not to just another woman; he had left Kali to move-in right next door with her friend.

Kali's mind is stressing to overcome her dilemma by painting a picture for the flipside of it. *What's the big deal! You did not love Joseph anyway. So, go get yourself a better man; you've got plenty of money to buy who or whatever you desire!*

Shockingly, Joseph's rejection of Kali has taken over her sound judgment. She doesn't want to be manless all of her life; therefore, Kali smiles as she gently whispers. "Yes, and I know just the man, Mr. Glen Monroe!"

Kali knows a man; without a second guess, he would belong to her forever. Especially when Kali is ready and able to pay out any amount for her to be this man's one and only. Kali questions her heart. "A bit insane! Is that really love?" Kali's mind seems to consider otherwise as it replies back. *What's love got to do with getting your man!*

For Kali this was true. For many years Glen was that man she wasn't pretty enough to entice, yet desires with every inch of her being. Relatively unlike Kali's issue, so many ladies want to take a ride on Glen's arm, but can't pay for his extravagant taste! As his price to play is a bit pricey: a Rolex, a Jaguar; just to name a couple. Though for Kali, what's a bit of money when she recently struck gold with an inherited amount of a few billion from her grandfather's estate? With an extra boost of green trust, Kali knows whatever she lacks in beauty, she'd certainly off-set with her billions! Mr. Glen Monroe will, without a doubt, be at her beck and call for a little loving.

Kali's mind was in conflict with her heart requesting. *Why not go after a man as Glen, who's so handsome and wanted by all the women? So many desire him, yet only the shades of your color of green can entice such a handsome man as him!*

Now anyone, who knows Kali Mathias, would never have believed she fixed her eye on such a good-looking man as Glen Monroe. Mostly; because Kali was not the prettiest woman in their community, but Glen is quite a ravishing fellow. He has a physique which locks hold of every woman's eyes making them want to explore every inch of his 5'11", tall and sleek well-built structure. His body appears to ooze in an extra layer of smooth, black licorice. Glen's facial profile exhibits such a sexy-manly existence that seems to oversee his clean-shaved oblong face outlined by a head of black, low cut, wavy hair.

Most women visualize Glen possess a few potentials which were worth all their fussing. He has these radiant brownish eyes; so, faultless and joyful. But, at that same time, eyes which seem to hypnotize your heart and steal your breath away at a glance. Useless to state; in spite of these many glorified wonders, Glen Monroe's heart was still for trade on an auction block to that highest bidder.

Kali was not taking any chances. She must be Glen's top contender on his secret ballot. Even if, Kali realized his price is a bit overrated for just an eyeful of ecstasy.

Kali never once asked herself, whether or not Glen's kind of store-bought love was even worth his steep tab. But, Kali was prepared to invest every penny which she had for just one passionate taste of Glen's warmth. For, she realizes most things, as with people have a breaking point where lust or money was involved. Therefore, her mind is convinced there is nothing wrong with buying a little love at a fair price from such a desirable man. Not once did she stop to consider if it's a sin to crave a man so that Kali made him more important than God. Kali's ready to purchase Glen at any cost without an ounce of regret.

Kali's self-esteem is too low to step aside and permit her essence to take a good view of her hunger for Glen; because of a few extra love handles. She's a few pounds on the fuller size; not what your typical man would ever consider beautiful or even cute, that is all her heart ever grasped. She never stopped; not once, to take a glimpse of herself thru God's eyes. Kali convinced herself at the early age of twenty-three, for her, to be the center of his world she must always be the one shoving out the cash.

Kali learned to use what she's never short of to get a man to take a second eyeful; money. The more cash she lines a man's pockets with, the more he desires her love and affection. Because the more loot she dishes out, the more attractive Kali thought she became before a man's eye. Even if this theory didn't work for Joseph Carlson, Kali was, without doubt, it will work for Glen Monroe.

With Joseph Carlson finally washed out of her brain. Glen has become the focus of her heart. She has set her eyesights on Glen. For Kali, the mission of bagging him has become infectious to her. Suddenly, Glen's that one man she must have in her life. She's played this game of chase with Glen, for so long; in her mind, he had seized Kali's soul.

Glen has become embedded underneath the roots of her skin. And, at that moment, her mind wants Glen anyway she could get him; for sale or hire; since it was a bit of love off the shelf.

Besides, with a lifetime invested of desiring this man whose core could never be hers. Kali made a pledge not to ever permit her crazy heart to fall in love with Glen a Don Juan. Given that, Kali is ever ingenious enough to attract him into her bed. Also, Glen was the man of her shameless cravings; not of Kali's heart. But still, she has to keep reminding herself, that Glen was merely not the loving type of man. Anyways, not the man for her heart to behold after the heartbreaking episode with Joseph.

Glen; the one man, who Kali desires so badly to be a part of his world. When knowing she's only going to be Queen Fool of his life. But for Kali, it's ok! Even if, she refused to believe the essence Kali rushes after is purely temporary. Because for Glen, a woman's love was just a seasonal thing. Never in his game plan with a woman to be a long-term mate. However, in Kali's soul, she never believes Glen couldn't, someday, be the long-time lover her heart has prayed-for. Even if; Kali's heart was a tiny bit unsure over the years with such gossip circulating of his reputation. Still, her lustful side need to have a piece of Glen. Kali's hungriness for a man is so intense she is going to pursue Glen with everything within her soul to make him her's lock, stock, and barrel. Glen is suddenly becoming Kali's drive for living her day. Each breath of air she takes has become labored with alluring him.

With thoughts of conquering Glen racing thru Kali's

head, this has been an extra busy week for her. So busy, she'd lost sight of Martha Hayward's surprise 40th party. Kali is suddenly giftless and thought she'd kill two birds with one stone. Kali figures, why not seize this occasion to entangle Glen's heart into her web of passion, and at the same time buy Martha a gift at Hay-Way Market.

Glen Monroe's the manager of the Hay-Way Market chain. Today as she cruises thru his market, Kali tries to get a bit more intimate with Glen. It has been two years since Kali moved to Virginia and it was more than time.

Kali was prepared and ready with nearly two years of plots in mind for ensnaring Glen with his own demons; money. She artfully smiles, saying. "A bottle of his most expensive champagne in the store. Well, this will have a man like Glen aroused, and quite an eye-catching gift to give my friend, Martha Hayward, for a present."

It was such a sure-fire scheme Kali's been perfecting for attracting Glen before Joseph swiftly popped in and out of her life. Joseph might have slowed her hunt, or it might have helped it along. Kali's timing could not have been any better since she has more capital than Kali has ever seen before. All of a sudden, she's alone with all of her cash in a changing lifestyle that's shifting before her eyes. Kali's going from rags to riches in just the blink of her eye with no one to share all her dreams with.

However, her newly discovered prosperity is not just money, but it comes with a climb up the societal ladder.

Kali becomes the life of the party as her empty calendar rapidly overfill. Kali's now receiving an invitation for all the elite group's private events.

A status in their neighborhood, which Kali adapts to wearing rather well. Because she knows gaining clout in such an influential community means getting noticed by Glen; as well as, more leverage to her plots.

Kali's awaiting scheme plays nicely into her hands. It was a Sunday, and all nearby liquor stores are closed, so timing presented itself ideally. After all, how would Kali possibly go empty-handed to a society gala of the times!

Glen's market was the nearby place for Kali to shop. Upon entering the store, Kali observes Glen at the cash register talking with a customer. As Kali sashays up and down the aisle, her mind starts to remind her of the old cat-and-mouse chase. This game which children used to play during their puppy-love stages as the little girls sent cute notes to the boys. Well, as grown-ups, it's playing a little hard to get, yet at the same time accessible.

Kali giggles slightly, "Umm! That old cat-and-mouse game. Oh, boy, it's been years, yet I still remember how to play it so well!" She dawdles a little longer in the aisle to look at the labels on Martha's favorite bottle of Dom Perignon. Kali was waiting for Glen's customer to leave his register before choosing this arrangement of elegant roses then going in line. Kali was still trying to boost up her nerves a bit so she could flirt with Glen and pick-up a date for Martha's high-class gettogether. Kali's certain such a handsome creature like Glen need not be on any guest list. Why would anyone oppose; not even Martha?

Martha's first love was money. However, her second

weakness was she loves the attention received from any man. And, of course, the more junk this man is packing in the trunk, the more eye appealing he was to Martha's taste bud. Glen will surely soothe Martha's palate nicely since he seems rather high-end. Still if not, Glen is quite a captain of his ship and breath taken at the same time.

Martha's guest list invited no one, whose greenbacks were not somewhat higher or; at least, equivalent to her swank lifestyle. Martha's the socialite of this small town. The who's who of Springfield and the beautiful Popular Club Leader of the pact for all the in-crowd of society.

Martha is a gorgeous woman standing 5'7" who was encased in a coffee tone complexion with flowing black hair down to her butt. Martha's face always radiate with such enthusiasm. Especially when her lips were gushing on the move with all the latest on Springfield, Virginia's communal gossip stories. Nevertheless, Martha was still one of Kali's old friends and neighbor. Kali must get an overpriced gift, or her name would be mud in their little cul-de-sac community. So, she continues shopping thru the aisles of Glen's market for his entrapment goodies.

Chapter Two

$\mathscr{K}$ali nears Glen's register carrying her bribes in hand to entice him. Kali passionately smiles while placing her flowers and shopping cart on the glider belt. He quickly glances skyward into her face for a split second quoting their store's dull slogan. "Welcome to Hay-Way Market! We hope you found all acceptable today." He lazily lifts her bottle of champagne out of this small cart placing it on the belt, then putting the handcart aside.

Casting his eyes back to his register, Glen recognizes he has seen Kali before today. Although, today he spent a little extra time with her at his register as his eyes were focusing on her costly items which sit before him.

Kali insists on trying to seduce Glen as she entangles his full attention by flashing a little of her money before his eyes. She's working hard yet at the same time he has no time for her idle chit-chat. Well, at least, until Glen's mind has finished with the calculating of Kali's financial wealth. The dollar bills were raging about in his brain as a permanent image of this black card brands away at his thinker summing up Kali's total financial worth.

Glen isn't basing her life's value on the two-hundred

dollar bottle of champagne nor roses. Glen's greedy eye was fixated on Kali's payment with her Black American Express Card. Glen's heart sings from that cha-ching of the cash register as it devises the games of his revenge.

A talent or curse, Glen has not figured it out. But his snout has become somewhat clever when sniffing out a well-off lady. Glen can sum up the assets by listening to the tone of their speech to the glittery jewels that adorn her neckline. He's not nicknamed *DollarBill Calculator* by the fellows without a purpose. Glen's the envy of all the guys in Springfield to have such a useful skill for getting the ladies. And, right about now, it's the hunting season for Glen's succeeding lady as the present one was about to exceed her seasonal dating statute.

Glen has projected Kali's net worth close to a billion dollars, and that is more than enough for his games. He is now ready to schmooze up Kali and her money a bit.

"Why helloooo beautiful! My name is Glen Monroe, and I am the Store Manager here." He beams sinfully at Kali. "Did you find everything you needed today, or did you forget one thing?" Of course, Glen was referring to himself as the forgotten item in her shopping cart.

Batting her long sexy eyelashes, Kali teasingly laughs as she glances into Glen's eyes uttering. "You could not possibly be referring to yourself as my missing object?"

Kali keeps on playfully trying to lead Glen on, as she returns his scandalous smile followed by a sexy wink.

Glaring nonstop into her face, he licks his lips a little before expelling. "Well, from the looks of your bag, it is a bit empty when I'm available in twenty minutes!"

Eloise Epps MacKinnon

Kali turns her face slightly away from Glen's view as she does a bit of math of her own on the subject. Kali's smiling inside as she has Glen's interest in her peaked at the exact stage where she wishes him to be. His eyes are faithfully in love with her Black American Express card. With each jingle from the swipe of the card as it echoes ching-ching into Glen's ears from his register has caged his soul. Glen's brain is awestruck by his core's thirsting for Kali and her assets. Was it, in fact, Kali or that black plastic which has Glen eating out from the palms of her crafty little hands? She marvels to eyewitness the effects of the plastic yanking on his heartstring; with every pull and tug, she deviously reels her big fish inward.

Finally, she gazes back into Glen's spellbinding eyes, uttering gently. "Such a shame! The timing is wrong for us both because I'm off to my best friend, Martha's 40th Birthday party!"

He grins, "Well, perhaps you would like an escort?"

She warns herself to go slow; not to pull Glen in too fast. She smiles. "Sorry, it is by invitation only. Perhaps, next time if you are available," she rapidly casts her eyes away from his view. She recognizes just one glance into his mesmerizing face, Kali can see the effects of that bit of black magic. She realizes he's almost her's. Kali grins while thinking within. *What a pushover he is! It just might be easier than I have imagined all these years. I cannot believe that I waited so long when it's like taking candy from a baby.*

Kali anticipates her next move a minute while Glen's mouth continues dishing out these complainants to her. His eyes are in like with what's in sight. For Glen, Kali's just a tiny portion of his prize. Because with all her cash a man could easily overlook a woman's modest qualities for a short period. At that point; all his eyes were seeing is beauty. As Glen leers at her figure, his eyes are noting nothing but loveliness. Kali's massive bankroll has Glen viewing her thru a pair of rose-colored blind folders.

Kali thinks to herself. *Quite remarkable how a little green colored paper makes even the homeliest things appear beautiful.*

Kali is observing first-hand the effect it has on Glen; especially after she sees him calculating her net worth in his head. Now he is visionless of the little extra baggage around Kali's middle section; her pair of love handles.

Kali's face wasn't what a man would openly consider unappealing. However, a few extra pounds which clung around since her adolescent years are making a man see her otherwise. Besides a few extra love handles, she was a bewitching woman, who was born without life's fewer qualities for most men. She's a bit homely but not ugly.

Even if, most men believe since she's a fuller figured woman who stands 5'5" that she lacks a dash of beauty, but not Kali. She possesses this appealing quality which neither Kali nor any man could see in her, only God.

A prettiness that soulfully conceals a pale sometimes whitish skin that's blemish free layering a roundish face. Kali has a few extra pounds of sensual body beauty that she allows, most often, to shelter a full set of lips which bear such a generous soul within. Though, due to Kali's heart's absence of self-love, it stripped her pair of joyful almond-shaped, hazel eyes of grasping her own beauty.

Whether Kali is pretty or not he was not about to let it affect his plot for revenge. Though, viewing Kali thru his rosy visions filled with her beauty and money before his eyes, Glen's a bit confused. Suddenly, he isn't sure if it was Kali or all of her cash that interests him so much. He flashes an edgy glare as he flirtatiously utters. "Well, the pages of my little black book shows I'm free for the rest of the evening." He hesitates for a second to search Kali's eager eyes. Glen smiles as he tries to ensnare Kali with his invite. "Just saying, in case your night becomes available a little later. Maybe, a little late-night snack and a movie?"

Staring into Glen's begging face, Kali devilishly grins while slipping her well-manicured, slender fingers inside her Coach bag bringing out a business card. Leaning on his register, she slips this card into his shirt pocket. Kali winks, "Maybe, I just might be available a bit later!" She gently pats him on the pocket as she flashes a sexy grin.

Then, Kali slowly bites her bottom lip as she sinfully fires a come-get-me-smile in Glen's path. She's working hard to snare Glen into her monetary web of seduction, and he is obeying Kali's every command.

Glen touches his shirt pocket as he slightly glides his hand over the area where Kali's business card rest, then he stares her in the eyes, sinfully boasting. "I'll certainly be using this tonight," as he removes her card to read it before he continues! "Miss Mathias, you can count on it for sure." He fires Kali a sensual wink while grinning.

Kali beams at him uttering, "It is the reason I gave it to you!" She grins, "I normally don't give such personal information of mine out to just any-ole body now."

Glen fervidly laughs as he jots his phone number on the back of the store's business card. He softly inserts it into Kali's right hand saying. "Honey, rest assured these digits will certainly be under a lock-and-key of my heart for you!" Glen's stroking the strings of Kali's heart with every ounce of charm he possesses to win Kali over for his next seasonal woman.

Glen's eyes were beaming like a lightbulb because he knew he had struck a gold mine. He didn't realize it was him being wrapped up in the web of riches, or probably it's Kali who is being ensnared. Because the way he sees it, she was his possession, not this other way around. In reality, Glen believes he is her pursuer, not Kali chasing him. He would never allow himself to be caught up in a woman's game of cat and mouse; he has no time for no "*Damsel in a Distress*" situation. He is that man-in-charge at the helm of his ship; no woman will control him.

Satisfied, he begins to look Kali up-and-down as she grins at Glen. Becoming a little self-conscious, she pulls her jacket together to conceal her middle section a little more from his view. She's trying to hide those few extra pounds that seem to bulge out from beneath her blouse yelling, "Helloooo! Look at me!" Kali swiftly looks over at him to notice if his eyes detected her little concealing action before she goes on. "I will be expecting your call about eleven or before if you get the least bit bored."

His lips form into a sensuous smile firing back at her as Glen quickly radars in upon Kali's self-consciousness from her few extra pounds. He senses with a few sweet lyrics and caresses; he could get her to believe she is the most beautiful woman who ever walked the face of this earth. Glen vows to himself once he puts a bit of loving on her tonight then Kali's merely one kiss away from all his. Glen's going to use what always gets his best results with a woman. He'll use his elegant way with words. He will flatter Kali with his charm. Mostly since the women visiting his store were not a prospect for his games. But becoming acquainted with Kali's prosperity today, Glen spotted his next lady for a playful game of love. Getting to meet a woman like Kali is like hitting a grand lottery.

Still glowing, he utters, "My place or yours tonight?"

"Neither!" Kali hurriedly affirms. "You only stated a late-night snack and a movie; nothing extra!"

With all of this flirtation, Glen was a little taken back by Kali's startling answer as his face seems a bit baffled. Glen rapidly affirms, "Helloooo; I was going to buy my favorite snacks here, and I figured there would be some movie on tv which might interest us." He frowns at her with serious eyes filled with inquiries.

Kali hopes Glen, her longtime investment, did show a tiny bit more class than he was portraying to her right now. He was not even trying to fake it as her mind drift off in thought pondering on his last words. *He's implying a cheap date or was he asking me to take a ride with him on that wild-side? To me, Glen's eyes were stating let's go straight to bed.*

Kali shakes her mind of any preconceived ideas then she glowers into Glen's face, asking. "Are you serious?"

"Why? Did you have something against a few snacks from here and a little tv?" Glen questions as he eyes her up-and-down a few times wearing this puzzled gawk on his handsome face.

With a leer of disapproval, she states. "Nevertheless, I should have realized only a booty call comes knocking after the hours of eleven when I extended the invite!"

Glen licks his lips a bit before saying, "Ohoo! That's certainly not my intention for this evening, lovely lady."

He was still playfully pushing her emotional buttons, stroke-by-stroke, as Glen winks at her dishing out a few more award-winning compliments to bait his catch.

Kali flashes a sexy smile, uttering. "Maybe we should table this date until you have a bit more imagination for this pretty lady!" Gradually eyeballing him, she picks up her bag slowly sashaying out of his store, not looking at him, or turning around as she forgets her flowers on his register. Of course, this was intentional on her part. Still part of Kali's trap to lure Glen in.

He could hear the swipe of the card going cold as he watches her walk away. Then, his eyes spots the flowers Kali had left sitting on his register. Glen hurriedly picks up this arrangement and begins a mad dash behind Kali bellowing out. "Miss Mathias, please hold on a moment you forgot your flower arrangement at my register!" He catches up with her; breathing hard, Glen strides beside Kali toward the car as he proudly carries her flowers.

Approaching Kali's car, she starts to place her bottle of bubbly in the back seat when Glen realizes she could be slipping thru his hands. He recognizes he must add a few more attractions to his game if he's going to get the attention of this woman. After all, she holds all of these acceptable assets he desires to be better acquainted with so Glen's lips fires off. "How about tomorrow night?"

Securing her bottle in the car, she turns about gazing into those begging eyes, as she laughs. "What about it?"

"Well!" He laughs. "After I get off work, I will come to your house to pick you up for a real date?" As Glen's alluring eyes leer into Kali's eyes, he tries hard to bypass any possibilities of Kali getting away. "What do you say, a quiet dinner for two at an elegant restaurant with a bit of soft music and candles?"

Fervently laughing, Kali utters. "Well, it appears, you are a gentleman, after all! And, I do accept. Finally, I do have something to chat about with you later tonight. I'll call you when I get home with my address."

Glen transfers the floral arrangement from his hands over to her hands as he smiles uttering. "I'll be patiently sitting beside my cell phone waiting for your call even if it takes you all night." He stares into her face. "Until we talk tonight, have an enjoyable time at the party!"

Winking without uttering a word, she gets in her car, as Glen happily walks away wearing a smile.

Chapter Three

Walking away, he keeps glancing back to see if Kali's eyeing him as she drives off in her car. She didn't desire to keep glaring back when her world was finally starting to revolve forward. Besides in her essence, Mr. Monroe is practically all hers. Kali looking back will only suggest she's desperate. Even though; Kali was, it still is not any sort of lasting impression which she desires to sketch in Glen's head of her. Not when he is starting to fancy her a little bit. Kali wants to believe with her and Glen lastly together, they would partake of many day-to-day ardent smiles. Kali must have faith in her and Glen's life ahead rather than gazing back at something that didn't exist.

Glen returns happily to his cash register, thinking he has conquered his target as Kali drives off believing she was the victorious one. Kali is confident she has already purchased Glen's heart with greenbacks and with a little good loving he'll want her. Kali plans to influence Glen with her tempting kisses! A passionate stroke of her lips on his that'll arrest Glen's soul, steering his core to her.

Kali has it all figured out for securing Glen but did it

make her life any better-off. She rides off full of doubts for basing her joy on materialistic hopes and a man.

Despite the fact, Kali was a God-fearing woman, she had somewhat lost her faith and trust. Her soul believes God's timing for reacting to her prayers will be too late! Instead of letting the Lord do His work, Kali's cash has tiptoed headfirst. It's now the front-runner to secure all her heart's desires. A bankroll was now persuading Kali to toss aside her good intentions for a chance at love.

Kali's fleshly demands are taking control. Her lust of Glen's instant affections are becoming a driven force to all her needs, rather than God. Instead, she was taking a jaunt on the desired train of amour with a man who she knew will become as venom to her heart as Joseph was.

Nonetheless, Kali is willing to take that chance since she's too afraid of being alone. Yet, worst than being by herself, she doesn't want to be unloved or manless.

Kali has finally acquired all the things in life that she thought could make her happy. Money, the large house, influential friends, and that one man she dreamed was a lifetime-mate; Glen. She's happy, but did Kali have joy?

Kali's so naïve her new-found status was making her mind believe these assets was her joys of life. What Kali fails to know she was missing a joy that only God could bring to her; the love she had laid aside. How can Kali's essence crave for the loss of God's love when it's being seized by human wants of this world! Kali's heart hopes her money can buy what God was not blessing her with fast enough, and that was instant love.

Kali's always on the search for love. She never stood still long enough to gaze back on her blessings. Nor did Kali grasp such lustful happenings are untying her heart from God! Why wouldn't this heart, who once caressed such an inspiring love inside not want it back? A tender spirit that loves Kali unconditionally and calms her soul on those lonely nights when she's all alone. The joy, she will only regain from loving God; never fleshly desires!

Suddenly a few greenbacks have stolen Kali's morals of life. It would appear Kali has forgotten who gave her these living treasures. She must learn those values in life all over that nothing can take the place of God's joy! As Kali situates her body into the driver's seat for the jaunt across town to Martha's party, her thirsting heart grasps for more. Yet, an unyoked soul is satisfied with the love which she believes Glen can offer. Even though, she's a tiny bit overcome by his sudden expression of affection for her today. When just a few days ago, Glen acted like she didn't exist as Kali strolled up and down the market aisles; one-by-one, trying to get his attention.

Kali's heart grasp the fact Glen doesn't want her, yet she thought he would not turn down a night of passion. A little loving and his soul might actually come to know her and see Kali does exist. No longer would Kali stroll the aisles unseen once Glen taste of her passion fruit.

Just as Kali's car come to a complete stop in front of Martha's house, her cell begins to ring. Hastily grabbing her phone from the passenger seat. Kali quickly glances at this number flashing across the screen. Kali's ecstatic to see it's her sister, Lynette Wilson, on the other end.

Even though Lynette is only nine months older; Kali always gives her the respect of an older sister. Lynette is that one person who Kali trust to call when in search of sound advice on life's unveiling issues.

Lynette and Kali generally chat a bit later on Sunday. Kali's elated to view Lynette's name lit-up on the cell. A little sister desperately need some guidance and wisdom from her big sister and closest friend concerning Glen.

Somehow, before Lynette can say a word, she senses the enthusiasm within Kali as she laughs saying. "Hello, my sister!" And rightfully so, because Kali's thrilled for an opportunity to tell Lynette how her little chase game entangled Glen Monroe. Kali was so proud to share her tactic with Lynette of how she landed such a handsome creature. A prize worth shouting aloud for all to hear.

"Good afternoon, Lynette!" Kali eagerly utters while musing over Lynette's inner and outer beauty. *My sister's a graceful woman with a light-tannish skin tone that layers over a roundish small face. Lynette has a pair of large golden-brown eyes which enhances her beautiful look along with a full set of lips that were always smeared with red lipstick just like our mother's. And shoulder-length silken black curly hair, with a cute little pug nose.*

Kali's moment of gazing back in time is disturbed by Lynette's concerned voice blaring into the cell. "How is my sister? Is everything all right with you?"

Beaming Kali asks, "What's with all the questions?"

Lynette laughs stating, "I was just thinking of you."

Kali utters with such excitement, "Sister, I'm simply great, a matter of fact your sister is in seventh heaven!"

"Sis, calm down." Lynette roars. "Catch your breath! What or who shall I say have you so hyper today?"

Kali laughs, "Lynette, now what make you think this excitement is over a special someone?"

Lynette softly laughs. "Because Kali, you're about to detonate and that's the sure sign of a man somewhere!"

Kali chuckles while speaking slowly, "Sis, sorry I just got the attention of Mr. Glen Monroe." She inhales this long lungful of air before asking. "You remember Glen, the man I've been praying about for ages? Well, I finally have a date with him." Being a little selfish, Kali did not stop talking for Lynette to get a word out as Kali carries on. "Lynette, I have been pursuing Glen for many years now; so many, I even lost count." She tenderly smiles!

Jumping in, Lynette laughs, "That old cat and mouse chase, huh! Sis, I hate to ask if you've hit that Hennessy bottle along with Martha? Because that sounds a lot like something Martha would have you doing."

Kali roars, "Sis, you must be kidding! You do realize that alcohol and I have this love-hate battle going on. It tries to tempt, and I ward it off by the blood of Jesus!"

Laughing, Lynette remarks, "I'm a bit worried about you living this new-found life of yours. I pray this is not one of Martha's blind dates again! Kali, surely you must know that girl is crazy; especially her choice in men."

Kali frowns, "Sister, get real now because I am quite serious here! Now, you know Martha's choice of men, I am not even on their map's radar. Most of the men feel I'm not pretty enough to be part of their society page!"

Lynette laughs slightly, "Honey; last I knew Martha's taste buds included yours, mine and ours when it comes to a man. The girl has no shame as long as it has a third leg, able, and willing and it has nothing to do with looks of any kind."

Kali bellows, "Sis, I had no idea you were so familiar with Martha's diplomacy!"

Lynette still tickled, "We both know Martha has not changed. Martha has been the same since you two were back in grade school. Kali, you realize I have spoken to Martha; a few times over the years, about eyeballing my husband." They both laugh at Martha's expense.

Kali calmly declares, "Sis you have that right! Martha lives for all the extra pleasures of life and tonight will be no different. Lynette, it's her 40th birthday, and I bagged a few of her favorites. A bottle of expensive bubbly and roses." Kali's eyes are sightful to Martha's idolization of life's pleasures. But, difficult for Kali's sharp-eyes to see her own money-oriented likings when each lyric spoken from Kali's lips spelled desire. Kali's praises about Glen to Lynette was evident of that human appetite of Kali's.

Kali's eyes were invisible to the fact, she is becoming no different than Martha. Kali idolizes that same greedy needs which she could only see Martha loved so much.

Lynette inquires, "Kali are you still there? You know I am a bit concern about you. After all, you just ended a brief romance with Joseph." Even though she's worried about her little sister, Lynette wants to listen to more of Kali and Glen's debacle of a merry-go-round.

Kali bares her soul out for Lynette's ears. She laughs divulging, "Sis, just when I knew this hunt for Glen was over, he proposes some crazy night of a snack and tv."

Lynette roars, "I couldn't imagine what you did next for a cheap date like that one!"

Kali grins. "Well, I played this old forgotten register game and left my roses. After all that, I finally got asked out on a real date with him for tomorrow night."

Lynette sigh in amazement, "Sis, it certainly seems as though you and Glen had one hell of an afternoon! I do understand why Glen was a bit hesitant to ask you out."

Kali, not understanding her sister's reply, she queries Lynette, "Why would you say such a thing?"

Lynette softly expresses. "Hearing the verses roll off your tongue. Girl, I almost did not recognize if this was my sister or someone else chatting with me."

Kali jokes, "Okay! Don't you think your little sister's ingenious enough to handle Glen?"

Lynette smiles, "Kali, I have not seen you this keyed up in a long time; above all, over a man! It is nice to see you, rather hear you so happy, but please be careful and not let your new adventures cloud your heart of God!"

Kali doesn't wish to hear any pessimist lectures from Lynette. Not at the moment, when Kali knows her path of life is going rather well. She's overjoyed the direction it's going in, as she utters. "Sorry to hang-up but I must run now. As you called, I was just driving up in front of Martha's house for a party. And, I bet Martha's peeping out of her blinds trying to figure out who is chatting me up on the phone because she is so nosey! Kali giggles as she continues. "Sister, let's chat later tonight or perhaps tomorrow if I hook-up with Glen later. Love you!"

Lynette returns, "Love you too, now please take care of

yourself! Let's talk tomorrow night, I want to hear all about your date with Mr. Glen."

"For sure!" Kali says. "Will call to tell you about that risque date of mine with Glen." Kali roars with laughter as her sister, Lynette, joins her before ending their call.

Strolling through Martha's front door, Kali spots her quickly moving away from the window. Martha had just finished snooping on Kali still sitting in her car.

Kali is all smiles, as she sashays over to Martha while still bursting at the seams from chatting with Lynette as well as her date with Glen. Kali voices a hearty hello to Martha's guests while Kali focuses all the attention back on the birthday girl and her friend, Martha.

Martha frowns into Kali's smiling face demanding to know why Kali was the last to arrive at her party. "Why were you just sitting in your car when you were already the last guest to arrive?"

Soon as Kali opens her mouth to retort, Martha puts up a hand inquiring. "What shall I ask was so important you were so late, and when you lastly arrived you sit out there in the car for ages doing ...?" Martha's angry voice abruptly relaxes in mid-sentence. As her eyes spots, this oversize arrangement of beautifully mixed colored roses in Kali's hands. She asks. "Are those for little ole me?"

Not at all amused by Martha's fake acting, Kali gazes within her face. Smiling, Kali transfers an elegant crystal vase of roses with this prestigiously, gift-wrapped bottle of Dom Perignon champagne into Martha's hands.

Martha was so delighted! She swiftly plants a big kiss on both Kali's cheeks. Then Martha's face switches into the most pleasing smile while uttering. "You should not have! You must have spent a fortune on these gifts."

Kali realizes that was all an act on Martha's behalf as Martha loved every dime Kali had spent on her. Gazing into her face, Kali utters. "Martha, you know I wouldn't dare attend your gathering without your favorite items."

"Kali these are simply divine choices!" Martha glares across the room at the other guests uttering. "My friend is so thoughtful and knows my taste so well. Would one of you please hand her a glass of bubbly so we can toast this big day of mine with Kali?"

Kali's head starts to seriously ponder if her ears were hearing correctly. *Did Martha just ask one of her guests to get me a glass of bubbly? Well, it looks as if, after all these years, she did know Martha well; yet does Martha, really know her at all.*

Kali's heart finally begins to understand it wasn't her who Martha desires to know again, after all, these years. It was Kali's status as the new baller of Springfield!

Kali has always known Martha was a user. But in her mind, Kali believes she must play the best friend role to survive among the sharks of Martha's hoity-toity rank.

Chapter Four

*E*very smidgen of liveliness Kali had seems to slowly drain from her limp body. She's taken back by Martha's offer of a drink but plays along. Kali swirls about facing Martha playfully answering. "I'm afraid your drink offer must wait for your next birthday as I have a hot date!"

Martha's eyes become broad as she affirms. "Honey, with whom do you have this date since my friends were all booked up when I asked on your behalf?"

Kali is raging from these vacillating emotions tearing her apart inside from Martha's unfriendly words blaring in her ears. As these verses echo within Kali's mind, she finds it hard to see how Martha could sink so low. How did Martha part her lips to blurt out such secrets before her uppity guests about Kali's dating life?

For Kali, the words were harmful to her ego. But it's Martha doing what she does best. Using a subtle phrase to get under Kali's skin. Kali tries to control the tongue, but this rage takes over. Kali crossly glances in Martha's path affirming. "Martha! God did make other men who has no ties to your stuck-up social circle of friends."

Martha is speechless as Kali goes on glaring into this

blushing face before continuing. "And, believe it or not, this man finds me attractive enough to ask me out on a date!"

Martha's face drips of humiliation from Kali's words as she gazes at her little bunch of society friends stating. "Darling, I was simply inquiring who! I realize all of my male friends were attending other social gatherings, and not available. As you know, they wouldn't have possibly missed out on a chance to celebrate with me."

As the words trickle from Martha's lips, Kali realizes it's time to make these women suffer a bit as Kali glares around the room into those questionable faces. Bravely, Kali gloats, "I cannot be late for my date with Mr. Glen Monroe." Kali could hear a pin drop in that room as all the ladies' mouth hung open. Kali's sensing such hatred in the midair, as she shifts her eyes toward Martha. Kali smiles. "It is a great party, and I wish you a Happy 40th Birthday, but I have a romantic adventure waiting."

Martha rejoinders. "Well, we must do it again soon!" Her cold eyes were signifying otherwise to Kali. Martha smiles, yet her heart is regretting all these extra wrinkles her face must use to muster up that hater smile. Martha is trying so hard to ignore who Kali has a hot date with. She embraces Kali while slightly laughing. "Darling, it is such a shame you cannot stay longer! You've barely had time to enjoy any of the festivities with your friends."

Kali gloats, "Martha, it sounds fabulous but how can a woman keep a man like Glen Monroe waiting!" Kali's blushing face smiles as these lyrics vainly pours willingly from her tongue. Kali hurriedly rushes toward the front door feeling a bit agitated with Martha and her guests.

Rambling to her car, Kali starts to wonder what type of friend could Martha be when she voices such cutting words to her. Kali sits in the vehicle for a few moments to mull over her feelings before the short drive home.

Starting the car for her drive home, Kali tries to seek a bit of stillness. As her head sorts thru Martha's cynical verses, just a drive around the corner appeared so much further. While the car tugs along, her head starts to pain from the many unanswered questions she needed to ask Martha. However, Kali was scared of the real responses the ears might have heard from her best friend, Martha.

Kali takes in consideration during their school years, she and Martha always had a rocky friendship. But now Kali is balling and could afford to move in a prestigious neighborhood she and Martha's union was stronger. So, not until today, Kali never observed such an obnoxious side of Martha. Therefore; in Kali's core, she was a little puzzled by Martha's actions toward her. Mostly, since it was Martha, who sanctioned her membership into their elite community group. Yet, unknowingly when Martha indorsed Kali in the group, Martha had no expectations Kali's popularity; among her group, would escalate that rapidly. It has always been Martha's seat on that societal throne ladder. A position which Martha and her money have held, and now Kali is slowly ousting her.

Martha was no longer the highest baller of their elite community. Not only did Martha know this, but for her uppity friends to hear Kali gloating of a date with Glen; one her hands didn't set-up isn't favorable. Since Glen's that one man, the ladies of Martha's elite group, expects her to fix them up with. Nevertheless, Martha wouldn't or perhaps she couldn't. Though, Kali, whose prettiness was less than them all, pulled it off.

Kali's date with Glen was such a setback to Martha's ego. Martha's edge was fast wearing off among her elite group as she watches Kali suddenly stealing her clout.

Kali never imagined Martha was in competition with her. Nevertheless, it was that wake-up call Kali's esteem sought-after to find herself again. Kali finally recognizes a friend like Martha was not her best scheme for getting Glen. Kali gloats. "It was me; I got a date on my own."

Kali rides along still mulling over her day, as notions of Glen starts to dance about her mind. As these happy thoughts overtakes her heart, the phone begins to ring.

Quickly, Kali steers the car over to the curbside. She stops, reaching for her cell phone off the passenger seat as she softly voices. "Hello, this is Kali Mathias!"

Answering the call, she hears Glen's velvety voice, as he inquires. "Hello gorgeous, how is your party going?" Not hearing any response from her, he goes on. "This's Glen Monroe in case you are dying to know whose sexy voice is at the other end of this line! Glen lightly laughs. "Is this a bad time for you?"

Kali's brain was tied-up by the vision of his salacious lips moving while Glen's sexy voice travels thru the line to her thirsting ears. Also, Kali's a bit speechless by this impeccable timing of Glen's call. Laughing, Kali replies. "No, I was expecting your call. And, Glen, the timing is perfect; I was just leaving the party!"

Glen carefully listening to Kali's words about leaving her friend's party as he goes on, "Well, since you turned down my earlier date; maybe you will let me tuck you in tonight. If you share your address, I can be there before you even miss me at the other end of the line."

Kali responds to Glen's gesture, "Wow! Tucking me in? Now, that just might be worth exploring. I believe it is bedtime now, so why not tell me more?" She goes on fervently jerking Glen's chain just a little while longer as Kali tries to avoid revealing her address.

"Really!" Glen laughs, as he excitedly voices. "Good! Since I couldn't bear another moment to bypass tonight before seeing your lovely smiling face."

Kali's mind crafts a sight of Glen's sexy body oozing over with chocolate as he snuggly lays her into bed. She breathlessly speaks as she strokes Glen's ego a bit more. "I was eagerly counting down the very second until our date tomorrow, but I like your idea a bit more."

Glen kicks into a romantic mode, "Oh baby! I am so pleased we see things eye-to-eye." He fires a sexy laugh, as he passionately confirms. "Kali, I am packing what it takes to make you sleep similar to a newborn baby after a soothing, bubble bath."

Kali passionately utters. "And, just how're you going to do all of this because my tired body desire to know?"

Glen fervently continues. "First, I will turn on a little soft music while I gently massage you down with a little baby oil and lotion. Then I will seal the deal with one of Glen's passionate, good-night body kisses all over."

Kali is awestruck by Glen's tender frame of mind yet grateful he was not near her at that second as he tries to lure her into his night of passion. She feels a bit devilish and risky, as she replies. "Oh boy! You really know how to tuck a girl into bed! Appears you're quite masterful at what you do. Perhaps; I just might desire to give it a try, since I'm suddenly developing a case of insomnia!"

Glen eagerly replies, "Kali, I promise you when I am done tucking you into bed tonight sleep will be the least of your worries!"

Glen's words were so inviting to her heart, as he lays his poetry on a bit thick for a chance to dip his oil stick. How else will he gain Kali's trust and seize her interest?

And, for a reasonably smart woman, she's soaking in every syllable as Glen hypnotizes her with his tongue. It might have been the blow-out between Martha and her, yet suddenly Kali needs Glen even more. Also, she feels a need to justify her life for Martha and all her groupies. Kali must flash her and Glen's date before their spiteful faces. That way they will realize she has their man. Glen was every woman's desire but snared by Kali, for today. Kali's scheming has captured Glen on her own, without any set-up from Martha's resentful hands.

Now Kali seeks to get back at Martha for ratting her out to Martha's high saditty friends. She reveals her one prize; Glen, to watch Martha squirm a little. Arrogantly, Kali conceitedly grins as her needy soul sinks lower into a world of wickedness. A society teeming with Martha's tone of spite, and Glen's riveting web of words into her ears. A place where Glen's passion for words makes her jewels thirst for the familiar touch of Joseph's arms and Martha's words makes her seek Glen even more.

While Kali's mind brood over her life, she overheard Glen's voice hammering for her ears at the other end of the line. Glen was using all his charm to get an invite so he can tuck her into bed. He clears his throat, feverishly stating. "Kali, you do know we can continue our heated tête-à-tête face-to-face." Glen tries to be nonchalant, so not to rush Kali into revealing her address until she was ready. But just the same Glen was seeking for a little bit of loving himself tonight.

She knows Glen is fishing for an address, she laughs. "It's so kind of you to offer, but I will let the gentleman off the hook for tucking me in for the evening. That's if you give me a rain check for another night."

Glen chuckles, "Oh, so you're giving me an out!"

She gently laughs, "Yes, it appears like the lady thing to do. Besides, I have a proposal to wrap-up tonight for a meeting tomorrow morning at work."

Glen feels she's trying to back out of his invite as he replies. "Hum! So, it's going to be like that tonight. Just keep in mind I normally do not give rain checks but for you pretty lady I will make an exception."

Kali starts with a sexy laughter while trying to assure Glen that she'll make good on his invite. "Please realize how I'm regretting not being tucked into bed by you. A chance of a lifetime for such thrills I am missing out on tonight. However, your decision to reconsider your rain check will not go unrewarded." Kali zealously laughs, as she carries on.

"Unfortunately, I really must run since it is getting quite late, and I still have lots of work to do."

Glen's equally as disenchanted for their conversation to end. However, he's not letting Kali hang-up yet. Not without his one last attempt to find out where she lives.

"I'll pick you up about 7:30 P.M.," Glen tosses in his question in between his joking. "Now, your chauffeur is wondering what address shall he pick you up for dinner tomorrow?"

Kali quickly tells Glen her address as she prepares to hang-up. She asks, "Now, with the address detail out of the way. I hope it does not mean we will not talk before you pick me up tomorrow evening."

Adding in this pleasing tang, Glen avidly says. "Even if I did have these visions of tucking you in tonight that you spoiled by shooting me down. But nonetheless, you will certainly hear from me before our date."

Kali devilishly laughs saying. "I certainly hope so!"

Glen unhappily says, "Baby, you do realize this heart of mine is quite disenchanted that I won't be tasting the sweet nectar of your lips. Or, to listen to the sexy sound of your voice as you sing my praises all night long while I rock you to sleep!"

Kali's eager lips fervidly utters. "Glen, you're not the only one disappointed by my decision. But, there would be one variance to your story since it will be you singing my praises before the break of dawn."

Laughing Glen utters, "That appears hard to believe, for me, without a small sample of proof tonight, Kali."

Kali counters. "You'll have to take my word tonight, but it'll be your joystick thirsty to explore a bit further."

For once, Glen's seconds of desire almost made him forget the avenging plot with Kali's money as he lets go an airy sigh. "Whew!" Glen excitedly states, "It's getting a bit hot and pasty on my end. So, let's end the call until tomorrow. Perhaps, you'll be ready to put into effect all of those big words you're expelling out." Glen says as if he's in an overheated moment from the sound of Kali's steamy words leaping through the phone into his ear.

She laughs while saying. "Believe me, this is one chat I'm willing to finish before or during our date. But until the time comes, let this moment be a memory of me."

Glen laughs. "That's for sure! Now, just be ready for whatever comes your way tomorrow. Good-night!" His mind replays their tête-à-tête as Glen sees a side of Kali that's quite appealing to his eye. *I do enjoy the feisty woman who finds her way about a bedroom with ease. A heart stealer for sure; the sort of lady who make any man forget a taste for revenge.*

Chapter Five

Snapping out of his trance, Glen assures himself that inflamed spell which Kali has cast over his core will not work on him. Glen mischievously laughs as he searches his mind. He lightheartedly quizzes himself. "What kind of foolish man let any lady come before his own gain?"

Kali sits back in her car seat a moment to process all her excitement for one day. Suddenly, she has more fire in her walk than ever after that brief heart-to-heart with Glen. Continuing the drive home, Kali's core is swelling with a newly uncovered pleasure, as she switches on the car's engine. She mumbles. "Umm! The charming lyrics from Glen's tongue looks like that right antidote, which was vital to get my engine purring again!" Even if, she's still in disbelief about this tête-à-tête with Martha, Kali's soul has a new lively spirit. Kali's engaging conversation with Glen has her acting just like a fourth-grader whose heart is so unsure of her first real kiss. Still, Kali realizes even without any assistance from Glen tucking her into bed, she'll sleep like an infant. Also, at this same period, Glen relaxes back in his chair to mull over just what his meeting Kali meant to him. As it doesn't take Glen any time to realize Kali was that woman he'd been awaiting; his game piece. Kali was the only woman Glen had met whose love resembles the same intensity of that woman which now prevents his heart of knowing true love.

Glen realizes he's acting like a kid in the candy store. He has fantasized from that precise moment a woman's love broke his heart for a day of pure reprisal. A time in his life where he would meet the same character of lady with a thirst for him and a never-ending ATM machine.

7:30 P.M. THE NEXT DAY

He's anticipating a romantic date with Kali almost as bad as she has with him tonight. Mostly, because Glen's been boasting to his buddies about that big catch which he lastly landed. And, after just one night together she'll be the next chess prong within his game of love.

As Glen prepares to leave for his date, he's flying on cloud nine. Glen was assured the dreamy, poetic words, his lips were about to recite for Kali's ears were about a lifetime of heartaches dissipating. Poof, like that puff of smoke, Glen's hurt will disintegrate. But, he knows only if his lyrics can make Kali's heart become his tonight.

A sly smile quickly covers Glen's face as he gaits out of the door to his car. Chuckling to himself, Glen states boldly. "Let the romanticizing game commence!" As he gets into the vehicle, Glen's mind visualize the image of him with an armored truck driving over to Kali's house. Glen's lips formed such a bountiful smile as he pictures a love-starved lady who's not at all ready for his games.

Glen was still in deep thought as he brings the car to a stop in front of Kali's door. His eyes were beaming all over from the assets before them, as Glen sits to survey Kali's property a while. Glen breathes softly as he grins, "Kali's bankroll just keep getting sweeter and sweeter!"

All that his eyes were viewing, Glen knows a woman like Kali, he has one shot at gaining her trust. And, then all which Kali had would be his. It all rests on their date for Kali being a dream come true. He stridently sighs as Glen steps out of the car. Closing the car door, he halts to glimpse into the side view mirror for a last once-over of himself. He isn't risking any chances of him spoiling a date with the next seasonal; Kali Mathias. He skillfully sighs with self-approval uttering. "Yes, I'm a prize from the very top of my wavey head of hair down to this pair of polished, shiny wing-tip shoes." As he walks forward with such self-assurance, Glen treads up Kali's pathway. Glen hurriedly frolics up Kali's set of steps leading right up to a staircase to her heart. He impatiently pushes her doorbell. Then Glen moves aside wearing a goofy smile while feeling an uneasiness to what his eyes is expecting on the other side of that door. Although, Glen couldn't see Kali's appearance as being anything less than homey appearing in the doorway as he impatiently waits for the door to open. Glen smiles while telling himself to make the best of whatever lemons were tossed in his way this evening. Since Kali's date is essential to his game plans.

As Kali opens the door, Glen's silly smile grows into that glowing stare of amazement. Glen's eyes were truly spellbound by an elegant woman who answers her door wearing a modish low-cut, red knit attractive dress. Her outfit was not see-through. Yet, Glen's eyes focalized in on every captivating curve of a well-rounded full figure.

Glen's speechless. At this moment, his heart appears to stop cold, as his eyes were in love with the woman in red. For the first time in his life, his heart was feeling an unfamiliar vibe. It is strange for him to see a woman for who she really was without all Glen's heartbreak leaping before his eyes as he now saw Kali. Glen is confused by the unexpected direction his heart is wandering down at that moment. A pathway Glen did not believe he'd ever travel again as his eyes becomes fervently obsessed with Kali. Glen's brain considers. *How's it possible for Kali to be the same woman who occasionally shops at the marketplace?*

His eyes were no longer seeing Kali as the unalluring lady. For what Glen's eyes were detecting was so similar to an ugly caterpillar who magically transformed herself and emerges into a beautiful butterfly. Glen's essence is astonished by Kali's gorgeous transformation tonight as his unbelieving eyes stands before her in the doorway.

Kali smiles as she utters. "Hello Glen, you are just in time! Please come in." As Glen steps thru her doorway, his eyes continue to look her up-and-down; he's in total disbelief. Was this woman afore his eyes really the same Plain Jane which he had seen around over the years?

Kali notices him checking her out, as she asks. "Can I get you anything to drink before I leave you for a few minute to touch-up my hair and makeup?" She stares at Glen smiling. "I assure you, I am almost ready."

Glen's eyes were so busy checking Kali out he didn't

hear one word from her mouth until she glowers at him repeating herself. "Can I offer you anything to drink?"

Glen laughs as he replies, "No, I'm good! Hopefully, you will not be long cause our dinner reservations are at 9 PM." He grins at her, "Besides, I think you look quite ravishing as you are!"

"Thank you, kind Sir!" Kali's eyes stare as she does a bit of dissevering of her own. Glen's a tad eye-catching. Smartly shaved, simply clad in this double-breasted gray two-piece suit. Glen reeks of her desired men's cologne Dolce & Gabbana Pour Homme that almost drove Kali insane. "I'll be just ten more minutes. I assure you since a person need not mess with perfection!" She flashes an electrifying smile at him while wickedly gloating.

Grasping the bait, Glen is letting that temptation get the best of him; he plays along with her as he shakes his head a bit uttering. "And, I see nothing afore these eyes but enchantment, so why take ten minutes, we could go now?"

Kali glances at him smiling as she thinks to herself. *I honestly must give the man his acclaim because he is as smooth as butter. And, so forthcoming with his compliments of me tonight. I wonder if he's trying to crack the code to my safe below the waist.*

Still gazing at him, she utters, "Well, then Sir, I guess it's settled. Then, why are we still standing here? Let me grab my things from the chair, and we can leave now."

Kali strolls over picking-up her purse and scarf from the chair near the door as he walks closer to her, saying, "You are looking and smelling good enough to eat right here with a knife and fork!"

Opening the front door, Kali slightly smiles as she is not

sure how to perceive his words. She gawps uttering, "After you Mr. Monroe because it seems you are a little hungrier than me."

Glen laughs. "You might be right cause I am hungry for that ravishing woman in red!"

Kali glares at him laughing, "I'm scared of you trying to woo me with your passionate lyrics. So, on that note, I know it's time to get some fresh air!"

Glen gazes at her as he leaps out of the doorway and hastily rotating around to take a second look. Glen tries to partake of Kali's beauty one more time before he has to share her with the public's eyes. In Glen's head, he is wondering if that was selfish or not. Even so, he wasn't ready to share that beautiful dream before him with any other eyes, except his own.

Glen is almost second-guessing himself as he probes thru his head asking himself. "Are these eyes misleading me? Was Kali truly the enchanting, beautiful vision that intrigue my spirit tonight?" At the second, he's not sure of the dream woman who beholds his every breath. For Glen, his feelings weren't about any deceitful games nor assets; not when his heart craves this lovely lady in red.

Although; Glen's eyes were hypnotized by the subtle effects which rest before them, he liked all he saw. And, Kali's red dress that outlines her body was just the extra added bonus for Glen's eyes since it's his favorite color.

Kali's sexy attire has Glen salivating at the mouth, as he says tenderly within. "What's Kali trying to do to me tonight? Kali's trying to drive me crazy wearing that red dress." Letting go the pressure, Glen tells himself. "Kali will never mess with my mind because it's strictly about the love games. Not a mind game about some red dress which could interfere with a scheme flow!" He breathes in a huge gulp of fresh air to cool down his libido.

Fervently standing behind Kali, Glen gets closer and closer to her. Glen's spellbound by the alluring perfume that entrances him as he waits for her to lock the door.

Glen is really trying to control these cravings for her, but his mind is filled with such curiosity. Glen's brain is getting the best of him as he longs to know what sweets he might find beneath such a riveting color. A color, he realized was not the shade of a green or lust; which was his real love. Yet still interestingly peaked with wonders.

Kali rotates around after locking her door. Glen was standing so close to her, Kali almost collided into Glen. Kali smiles in his waiting face as Glen moves down two steps. Glen smiles, as he holds out his arm for Kali.

As Kali grabs hold of his arm, Glen's eyes comb this affluent neighborhood where she lives. An aspiring idea begin to flow throughout Glen's mind of what it would be like to live here with Kali. He's confused by the heap of strange notions that excitedly races about his head as Glen's head ponder. *Was it because all of his heartbreak was dissipating or is Kali becoming more irresistible with every eyeful?*

He clears his mind while taking another look, as Kali fastens tighter onto his arm. Glen escorts her down this short pathway to his car as he opens the door for her to sit inside. Walking around to the driver's side Glen tries so hard to reason inside his heart. Why is seeing Kali so elegantly dressed messing with his sexual desires for her now? That delicious smell of Kali's body along with the impressive shade of red she is wearing was undoubtedly stirring up his libido. It was causing some kind of weird adverse repercussion on Glen's mood for retribution.

Kali laughs to herself as she sits in his car waiting for Glen to pace around to the driver's side and get into his vehicle. Kali could plainly see through the devilish smile on Glen's face that she's his choice for dessert tonight."

As Glen opens his door; positioning himself into the driver's seat, he avidly gazes over at Kali gently uttering. "Kali, I must say you really do clean-up quite nicely!"

Kali's face lightly frowns as she asks. "Glen, was this a compliment or should I be insulted by your words?"

Kali notices the way Glen's eyes were glancing at her lustfully. Yet she thought it was because he enjoyed that new look of hers which she had slaved hours under hot hair dryers and with a makeup artist to accomplish.

Glen knew, even without her bringing his blooper to his attention. He recognized how the words might have been heard by Kali's ears soon as these words rolled off his tongue. Glen wishes that the words could have been rephrased, but they were already spoken. He sees a look of displeasure smeared over Kali's face. Glen senses the need for a little charisma to get him out of this slip-up.

Starting his engine, Glen glances at her saying. "Why would you think such a thing? These eyes have not seen anything as lovely as you are tonight for so long and the red dress is quite tastefully worn." His eyes were radiant as he turns to her passionately saying. "You are a vision to behold tonight Kali, so beautiful!" As the words flow from his lips, Glen was just as surprised to say the lyrics as Kali's ears were to hear these words from his tongue.

At that very instance, Glen recognizes himself doing and saying things that were not like him at all.

Slightly biting on her bottom lip, Kali feverishly says gently, "Well, after such a lovely melody of words. How could my ears miss your first compliment?" She leers in Glen's big brown soulful eyes stating. "Thank you, kind Sir!" In Kali's mind, she figures Glen's starry-eyed lyrics were all part of her being his dessert for this evening, as she gazes at him thinking. *I got your number tonight, and it's not going to win any prized treasures from this love nest!*

"Whew!" Glen tenderly sighs within as he gazes into her eyes for a minute feeling he has won the round with his slick play on words. He grins, "I mean every spoken word from these lips, you do look fabulous!"

Glen's face is glowing as his car pulls away from the curb. He was off to wine and dine, Kali, tonight to such an enchanting date that she will be pleading with him to come take of the treasure chest and rob her blind.

Chapter Six

Glen and Kali rides along in his Lexus barely hearing the notes of the smooth jazz playing in the background.

Both Glen and Kali's mind were preoccupied on the faraway escapades which still awaits to be discovered by them tonight. As these exotic, vivid images of her frolic thru Glen's head making him want her more-and-more. Glen knows he must rid the mind of the notions before he pulls over and lay an avid kiss on Kali's waiting lips.

Glen couldn't understand what was wrong with him. He believes a bit of mild conversation was crucial in the air to calm his libido as he softly inquiries. "Do you like seafood?" He laughs, "I realize it's a fine time for me to ask, but I have selected a quaint little romantic place for us to dine. And, it has the best seafood in town."

"What's not to like about seafood?" Kali looks in his path as she quickly comes back. "May I ask where?"

Glen laughs, "Well, I have said enough already. How can this be a surprise, if I spoil it by telling you where?"

Kali laughs as she says. "Well, I hope this surprise of mine is not much further because I'm starving."

Glen utters. "Be patient, it's right around the corner. And, I think the food will be well worth your wait."

Soon after the words escape Glen's mouth, he steers the auto off the road down a little winding path. Swiftly his car comes to a stop before a little charming Seafood and Steak Restaurant. Glen laughs as he gawks across at Kali sitting impatiently in her seat, saying. "Well, we are here, and you will see it was worth the suspense."

Kali laughs! "I certainly hope so as the place appears charming and does have a romantic flare about it! Now, until I taste this seafood, the jury is still out on that!"

Stepping out of the vehicle, Glen dances around and open Kali's car door. Extending the arm, Glen and Kali avidly glides into the restaurant together.

Inside the front door, Glen strolls over to the young woman at the Reservation Desk. Glen lovingly smiles at her while boldly sanctioning. "Hello, I'm Glen Monroe, and I have reservations at 9 P.M. for two."

The young lady quickly gives Kali a once over as she winks at Glen saying. "Yes, I'll check on that for you!"

Just as Glen starts to speak with Kali, the young lady returns with a friendly smile uttering. "Yes, Mr. Monroe I do see your dinner reservation for two. And, Mr. Milo should be along momentarily to seat you and your guest at your preferred table before long." Mildly smiling, she blushingly sneaks Glen a suggestive wink.

Glen slyly smiles at Kali while casting his eyes out of the young lady's path, uttering. "Sure, that will be fine!"

Then, Glen stares at Kali sheepishly laughing, saying. "I have been here a time or two, as you can see."

Kali notices, it's a bit awkward for Glen as it was for her. He plays it off by continuing to smile. Glen glances at Kali to see the expression on her face before uttering boldly. "Food is so good, I even have a favorite table at this restaurant."

Kali grins while saying. "Yes, so I'm hearing!"

As the playful little rendezvous enacts between Glen and the young lady, Kali's eyes grasp every scene. Kali's surprised at Glen. But she's not about to allow a jealous hostess, who's harvesting a childish crush for Glen ruin this passionate moment. A date with Glen that Kali has played over-and-over in her mind for what appears like a lifetime to happen. So, Kali's not allowing anything or anybody to step in now and seize a long-awaited dream. Not when Glen's the only man Kali has ever loved who impassion her heart and soul just to be in his presence.

Although; Kali already affirms it takes more than the hostess's few fervid winks to keep Glen's devotion. She still disliked the hostess's lusty eyes keep swooning over him. Even if, Glen did have a track record with all these ladies, its Kali's time tonight. Kali looks over at Glen as her brows slightly lifts uphill while recognizing her part in this hopeless tug of war game being played over him. A man, who Kali knew didn't desire the hostess tonight to quench his thirst. Realizing this, Kali ardently inhales as she grabs hold of Glen's hand. Kali's heart was ready to let her guards down and start enjoying their date. She dazzles Glen with a sexy wink. As Kali gloatingly smiles at the hostess a friendly gesture confirming Glen was all hers; at least, for this evening.

Glen stands between the two rivaling women as they both demand his attention. But, as Glen searches about the room trying to catch Jameson's eyes, he glimpses an unsure stare on Kali's face turns to a satisfied smile.

Not sure what's next, Glen's wishing Jameson would rescue him from the clutches of the women before Kali gets wind of his past from the hostess.

For Glen, Jameson Milo is not only the owner of the establishment, SeaShore's Steak and Seafood but Glen's closest friend and go-to person. And, although Jameson doesn't possess the same flare or the extra sex appeal as Glen, he was attractive. Jameson is a stout fellow whose muscular physique appears to scream out, "Hello, come and get me as I'm available for the asking!" Not what is in the market for capturing the ladies eyes as with Glen, whose demeanor shouts with an air of self-assurance.

Glen's eyes finally see Jameson's cheerful face across from him. Glen's heart couldn't have been happier than right at the instant. Especially, since Glen's sensing a bit more tension than usual from Jameson's hostess.

Noticing all of these weird vibes, Glen's mind begins to reason with his absurd choice to bring Kali to a place where he has taken so many of his dates. *What was I even thinking to bring Kali here?*

Glen recognizes this place holds so many unresolved skeletons that still accumulates within these walls of the restaurant. All tongues of the workers here could reveal those secrets with the other women which he spoiled at SeaShore's Steak and Seafood. Some of Glen's secrecies in the cupboard; if Kali knew, might ruin his chances of introducing her to his class of love. A gamble that Glen could not afford to take, still he brings Kali here. Why?

Looking upward, Jameson catches Glen's eyes, as he cavorts over to seat Glen and Kali. Jameson's eyes were protruding out of their sockets, as he notices Glen's not swooning over one of his model type partners. Jameson gets curious as he grins while searching for a juicy story. "Good evening, Mr. Monroe! And, how is your evening thus far?" Glen smiles as Jameson nosily ogles at him.

Glen knows Jameson was fishing as he smiles saying to him. "Tonight, this has been one of the best times of this year! And I am looking forward to some good food to make it even better tonight!"

Jameson laughs, asserting "Well! Mr. Monroe, please allow me to escort you and your guest to a table. And, I must say the night will get even better because I believe today's menu has one of your favorites!"

Glen humorously laughing, he asserts. "Okay, please knock it off with the Mr. Monroe baloney!" Glen avidly slips his hand about Kali's waistline as he carefully pulls her closer to him stating. "Kali Mathias, this is Jameson Milo one of my best friends and owner of this delicious seafood restaurant."

Before Kali could open her mouth to utter his name, Jameson leaps forward saying. "It's always a pleasure to meet one of Glen's lady friends." His brain was musing about the reason why Glen wine and dine these women and wondering *what Glen's warped game plan for this one is?*

Kali's not entirely sure how to perceive Jameson nor

the words from his mouth. Kali keeps silent as Jameson escorts her and Glen around the outer parameter of the room to this romantic table. It was in a secluded corner near a large window overlooking an ocean view. Quite a romantic setting indeed. As Kali starts to think Jameson was privy to that scheme Glen had to woo her right out of her red lacey undies tonight beforehand.

Jameson begins to muse about these thrills of Glen's love life as he turns around to grab the menus. *What sort of love portion does my friend work on the women? Because seeing the Glen Monroe's life story thru my eyes, Rock Hudson certainly has nothing on Glen. Not with all these wealthy females which he parades on his arms in and out of my establishment.*

Returning his attention to their table, Jameson snaps out of those spicy tales racing about his head of Glen as he pulls out Kali's chair. His eyes gleam as he leers over at Kali while handing her a menu. Then he passes Glen a menu as he notes. "The Alaskan Baked Salmon is one of our specialties for the evening. And, Glen, I realize it is one of your preferred dishes when dining here."

Glen's forehead gets a few wrinkles as he glares over at Jameson affirming. "Thank you! It's one of the meals I do enjoy when I come here!" He turns to Kali stating, "Maybe we should try it tonight, it truly is delicious."

In Glen's mind, he's wondering why everyone at this restaurant has to air all his business out in front of Kali. Even his friend Jameson was not helping these matters. This was supposed to be Kali's date, not a time with his past women, who he had previously wined and dined in the same place. He wants Kali to feel like she's the only woman which he has ever romanced with at SeaShore's Steak and Seafood; sort of their special place.

Suddenly Glen's feeling a little closed-in as he shoots Jameson that time for you to just walk away stare.

Jameson picks up on Glen's clue for him to just step away as he states. "One of our waiters will be over soon to take your order." He gazes at Kali saying, "I do hope you enjoy dining with us tonight, Kali!" As Jameson felt Kali's just the one-night investment for Glen. Since she visibly lacks that beauty card of these women ballers his friend typically parades on his arm. Neither, Kali's facial or bodily appearance carry any clout next to the Marilyn Monroe qualities of Glen's sophisticated women.

As Jameson strolls away, Glen looks across the table in Kali's eyes. He fervently takes her hands in his hands as he effortlessly states. "I hope the start to this evening has not put a damper on your evening. Also, that I have made it perfectly clear there is no one, other than you, I want to be here with tonight."

Suppressing her feelings within, Kali fakes a pleasant smile as she replies. "Now, what makes you believe that I would think anything other than that?" She glares into Glen's face wondering. *Does he see naïve little fool written all over my face? Yet, I knew all the obstacles that I would encounter going after a man like Glen Monroe; Springfield's gigolo!*

Just as Glen parts his lips to respond, the headwaiter approaches their table interfering with the conversation. The waiter smiles as he says good evening to both Glen and

Kali while busily positioning a glass of water before each of them. The waiter carries on, as he adds a basket filled with assorted rolls and butter on their table. Done sitting up, he precedes to assert. "Good evening, thanks for dining with us tonight. My name is Thomas, and I'll be your waiter tonight." Thomas clearing his throat, his words take on a more staid tone as he asks. "Please, can I get either of you a refreshing cocktail or a fine glass of our house White Burgundy wine?" He winks at Glen!

Glen looks at Thomas saying. "I believe the lady and I will have a glass of Pellegrino sparkling water with just a dash of lemon and lime." As Glen eyeballs Kali's face, he confirms. "Of course, providing my beverage choice meets with the approval of my date?" He winks at Kali!

Kali says. "It is actually one of my preferred drink."

Done, Thomas asserts. "I'll give you both a moment to review the menu while I get your drink order filled."

No sooner than Thomas walks away, it appears he is back with the drink orders. As he sits their drinks down before them, he inquires. "Please, might I indulge either of your tastes with one of the mouthwatering specialties this evening? One of my preferred is the Baked Alaskan Salmon. It's seared in a creamy white wine sauce served along with a Baked Potato, Green Bean Almondine and a Side Salad of your choice."

Right after Thomas completes this one special, Glen stops him in verse as he gazes at Kali voicing. "I believe the lady and I will have this special, no need to go on."

Kali's a bit surprised Glen orders for her. Yet at that same time, her taste buds have been salivating for a tiny mouthful of their Baked Alaskan Salmon since Jameson mentioned it. Or was it this sensual man that sits before her, which Kali was cravings for and not the meal. Glen is looking quite appetizing as he sits across from her.

Thomas's eyes sparkle as he grins stating. "Excellent choice! You're both going to enjoy your selection."

When Thomas finishes writing their dinner order, he proceeds to walk away. Glen gawps at Kali as he affably speaks. "I hope you do not mind that I ordered both of our meals. Of course, you may have whatever your little heart desires, but I believe you will enjoy the special."

She replies, "Actually, I was dying to taste the special since it comes so highly recommended!"

Glen flirtatiously winks at Kali. He avidly grins while casting a warm and sultry kiss of passion in her path.

Kali flutters her long eyelashes at Glen as she begins to blush before fervently uttering. "Thank you, kind Sir! As our date is turning out to be quite lovely indeed."

Right then, Glen's unwilling heart was on a fast ship. He is floating hook, line, and anchor into Kali's path. A place he doesn't desire to be now or ever with a woman in his lifetime; not even Kali.

Chapter Seven

*G*len knows the only thing he desires from a woman was her to be his play toy for a little dessert. Otherwise, Glen's heart wanted no part of the drivel. Other than as a prong in his twisted games of love.

Glen's eyes gaze across their table into Kali's eyes, as his heart begins a bit of soul-searching. He answers her. "Good, because I planned our date for you; only you in mind, so I'm glad you are enjoying yourself!"

Kali's face is radiant, as she sits across the table from him looking into Glen's entrapping, soulful brown eyes.

Thomas sees Glen and Kali expressing a moment of passion as he returns to the table with the meal. Placing a plate before each of them, Thomas's face glows into a pleasant smile. Thomas moves to the edge of their table inquiring. "Is there anything else that I can get either of you, at this moment?"

Quite pleased with their choice and ready to indulge, Glen and Kali both counters. "Not right now, our meal looks delicious!" At that very moment, not one of them could anticipate them wanting or needing anything.

Thomas grins in both their paths as he says. "Please,

enjoy your dinner." As Thomas walks away, he senses a bit of heated passion in the air coming from Glen's side of the table. A part of Glen, he'd not noticed for any of the many ladies Glen has wined and dined there before. Thomas lingers a few moments to admire Glen ardently eyeballing Kali's beauty before smiling and walking off.

Kali sinks her teeth into the Salmon as she utters out to Glen. "The Baked Alaskan Salmon is to die for! This dish was a wise choice as it is cooked to perfection. Just the way I fancy my man, lip smacking and finger licking good." To her surprise, Glen lifts his left brow, as those words roll off her lips with such ease. With talk like that she must check to make sure her glass contains water.

Glen gazes over at Kali gloating. "I think it's cooked just for me. This Baked Alaskan Salmon is seasoned for soothing only my palate by our chef; marvelous job!"

Kali cuts an eye in Glen's path expelling. "I wouldn't be the least bit surprised as they seem to know so much about you here. Why not your taste buds, too?" Tickled by her own jibe, Kali lightly laughs as she flickers a sexy wink at Glen, who sneers at her, gloating. "Now do not be a hater, Miss Mathias!"

As Glen and Kali sits sharing a joke; out of the blue, Thomas returns to the table with an expensive bottle of champagne and two glasses. Thomas says as he starts to angle the bottle to fill up one of their champagne flutes. "Mr. Milo asked that I bring you the champagne. It was complimentary from one of our other dinner guest."

Kali sticks out her left hand stopping Thomas as she

gazes into Glen's eyes. Glen glares back into Kali's eyes while they both sits utterly speechless. Neither of them could think of anyone who would dare to send over the extravagant gift to put a damper on a heated romance?

Kali and Glen, appear to wear such inquisitive glares smeared on their faces as she silently waits to see. While his eyes rove around trying to make sense of someone's bad gesture. Yet, on the other hand, Glen just became a praying man as he starts to plead with God soundlessly. "Please do not let this be Jo-Ann!" Glen is dreading any thought of that person being Jo-Ann Parks. His current seasonal woman and lover. But Glen didn't understand; if that was Jo-Ann, why Jameson hadn't sent some kind of warning his way?

A bit nervous, he bites the bullet. Just as Glen opens his mouth to inquire, he overhears the unreceptive tone in Kali's speech. His lips closed as Kali's arduous words pour off her lips to Thomas. She insists Thomas reveals a name. "You've got precisely two seconds to tell us the name of this person who sent us that champagne or call Jameson over here? What's it going to be!"

Before Thomas could reply to Kali; who ordered the expensive champagne for their table. Martha slithers up to their table from around the corner slyly laughing!

Kali's veins seems to become red-hot with rage. Her forehead shoot skyward creating tiny wrinkles all across her face to grasp it was Martha. Kali's eyes doesn't want to believe who stands before them as she exhales loudly before requesting an answer. "Martha, why are you here intruding on my date-time?" Kali was spitting bullets, as she sits with fiery eyes glaring sternly in Martha's face.

Martha blushingly laughs as she answers. "Darling, is this anyway to receive your oldest and best friend? Such a foul-tasting greeting!" Martha cunningly smiles as Kali sits scowling upward into Martha's face.

In Kali's head, this question was running throughout her brain. *How did Martha track her down? Mainly, when she didn't even know where Glen was taking her tonight.*

Martha stands with a lost look on her face while Kali becomes angrier by the second. Even so, Kali grins and plays the role as Martha's devoted friend. Kali just can't run the risk of Glen seeing her; on their first date, going thru a meltdown. Somewhat peaceful, Kali asks Martha. "Why would you just show-up here tonight?" She stops before heatedly going on. "Better still, how did you find out I was at SeaShore's Steak and Seafood with Glen?"

Martha beams. "Oh Sweetie, you seem astonished to see me. But beloved, I must know before I answer your request. "Would this be Glen as in Mr. Glen Monroe?"

Glen could not imagine who's that bossy lady asking of his name. Glen sits silently while perplexity layers his handsome face. He goes on mutely listening to Kali and Martha's tête-à-tête about him while thinking to himself about Martha *that's one twisted and sick broad*!

Despite a glaze on Glen's face, Kali looks at Martha, she frowns. "The one and only, Mr. Glen Monroe. But; somehow, I'm certain you knew that without asking!"

Martha grins sinfully, as she ignores Kali while trying to get Glen's full attention. But even if Glen was fooled by Martha's games of charades, Kali was not. Not when

Martha is her go-to person, whose ears were the catcher of all Kali's secrecies. Even these hush-hush things Kali told Martha about Glen is caged in her mind. Excluding Kali's sister, Lynette, Martha was that only other person Kali trusted enough to say how she sits in bed craving a man, who did not know Kali even existed. Nonetheless, in the same town, but in the world. So, Kali realizes this absent-minded pretense Martha's playing is all an act.

Martha does know; all too well, who Glen Monroe is in the flesh. That is one of Martha's little dark secrets of knowing where Glen allures all his ladies; including Kali and her purse strings. She, not only knows who Glen is, but Martha's quite acquainted with his repute as a ladies man. Since this Glen, Martha knew, he would glide thru a woman's heart similar to a cold stick of butter melting in a hot skillet. Also, Martha recognizes that was Glen's romanticizing style of harsh and lustful love; not Kali's.

Glen, she did know. But, not how the twisted games started with a broken heart. A bit of despair that rapidly turned so wicked for Glen and the women in his world. A place that belong to Glen which had no way out; not unless he releases your heart and soul back to you. That flirtatious voracity of Glen's brain for the twisted shade of green was controlling his heart. The enemy disguised itself as actual love in the form of an enthralling time of deception. A playful cycle of trickery which leaves these women; Glen fantasizes to love, all alone and harboring this broken heart in the end. Because once this seasonal time of Glen's deceit stop, so did the love. As Glen was not bent on ever retelling that same old story twice with a lady who knew how to play a twisted shades of green.

Well, that's the writings of this scandalous Glen who Martha thought she knew. And, the one man who she'd prevent, however necessary from breaking Kali's heart.

Even if this meant Martha has to tell a few white lies to keep Glen's madness away from Kali's heart. Mainly, because Martha knows Kali is searching for a good man and the Glen, she remembers, was probably not him.

Yet, as Martha sees him seated across from Kali, she senses a certain maturity about Glen. Martha observes a more appealing man sitting cross from Kali as she starts to self-consciously question her own judgment of Glen. As Martha rumors within. "Was the fear for Kali dating Glen wrongfully presumed on his sorted past or mine?" Just as Martha's words ended, she sees a spark on Kali's face which didn't rest on Glen's. Then, Martha was sure Kali's core needed defending from an unreturnable love style of Glen's. Yet; at the same time, Martha hopes she is wrong about Glen's genre of love for Kali's sake.

Kali sees a mystified daze flickering in Martha's eyes, as Kali edgily probes. "Martha, who are you dining with here at SeaShore's Steak and Seafood this evening?"

Martha grins at Kali emphasizing, "Beloved, I was in this neighborhood and hankered for a bite of delectable seafood." Martha quickly yanks a chair around from the nearby table, as she signals to her other partner in crime to run along home without her. Then Martha glances at Glen saying. "I'm sure you agree it's our best seafood in town or you wouldn't be wining and dining Kali here."

Glen grins as he turns away from Martha's view, and affirms. "A matter of fact, I was telling Kali that precise same thing on the way here. The seafood is delicious!"

Kali casts an evil eye at Martha when her mind starts to become curious about Martha's motives. Kali broods over this matter as she whispers within. *"I wonder what is Martha's game plans coming here tonight? I'm sure Martha must have a few tricks up her sleeves to ruin my date with Glen.*

Abruptly, Kali overhears Martha's scheming laughter as she notes Martha flashing a sexy wink in Glen's path. Gawking into Glen's face Martha outstretches her hand before Glen's lips as she awaits him to kiss it.

Glen couldn't imagine what this woman is expecting him to do with her hand thrust before his face. He leers straight into her face admiring the beauty but marveling who she was and if she's lost her ever-loving mind.

Seeing the glower on Glen's face and his questioning eyes, Martha hastily draws in her hand. Without a word, she flamboyantly introduces herself after recognizing he did not remember her. "Hello, I'm one of Kali's dearest friends since childhood, I'm Martha Hayward!" Martha stretches her hands across the table touching Glen's left hand before going on. "Silly little old me! I'm quite sure Kali has talked so much about me, already."

Although the three of them were sitting in that same room, their minds were miles apart. Both Glen and Kali were waiting and watching Martha as she dramas out all her shenanigans. However, Martha's head was racing all over the place trying to know Kali's new Glen and what games he was playing. So, only Martha knew the reason she was at the restaurant tonight; not Jameson, Glen or Kali. As the three of them plays Martha's waiting game.

Suddenly, Martha deviously lets out a strange cooing sound, as she squeezes Glen's left hand a bit cozier into her hands. Martha startlingly exclaims. "So, you're Glen Monroe!" She sits ogling in Glen's face avidly smiling.

Glen's wondering if he knows this Martha woman as she sits fondling his hands and glorifying his name with her lips. He quietly asks himself. "Was that woman one of my past lovers?" Lightly smiling Glen is unsure as he releases Martha's hold on his hands, asserting. "Martha, how nice to meet you! And, I'm sorry to say Kali hasn't mentioned your name; not once, all night!"

Martha tries to make-believe she didn't hear Glen as her eyes circle around the dining room looking for their waiter, Thomas. Catching Thomas's eye, Martha signals for him to come over to the table.

Approaching Martha, Thomas notices the shifty eyes rolling in his path as her tongue rumbles. "Beloved; fast now, go bring me a menu and another champagne flute for a smidge of bubbly since my mouth is parched from all this confrontation here!"

Gazing at Martha, Thomas retorts. "I'm sorry to say, but the kitchen will shut down in thirty minutes. I could see what the chef has to make you a nice sandwich."

Martha frowns at Thomas averring, "Darling, a glass to share some of the champagne with my friends would be quite lovely! Now, if you could just go away and take care of that one thing for me!" Rotating about, Thomas bumps into Jameson. As Jameson eagerly awaits behind Thomas; so proud, with a flute for Martha in his hands.

Jameson is smiling from ear-to-ear as Martha's voice mesmerized him. Martha's sensual, yet familiar, laughter is detectible anywhere. The avid tone that once soothed Jameson's ears night-after-night with such sweet words.

The melodious sound of Martha, Jameson knew will always be familiar. For him, her sexy voice will continue to pull him in closer-and-closer with every spoken word Martha sings. No different than Martha's tone tonight.

Jameson spots such a radiant adore on Martha's face as he beams thinking it was for him. But, as he sees this way Martha's eyes swell up when she views his bottle of expensive champagne. It wasn't long for a hopeful man to recognize Martha's classy taste was admiring a bottle; not the man. That one man who remained wishful after fifteen-years, and sent the bubbly sitting afore Glen and Kali. A prank on his best friend; Glen, for Martha.

Chapter Eight

*M*artha's heart realized when she called Jameson, he might still desire her love. A place within Martha's core she wasn't willing to explore with Jameson. Particularly, when fifteen years ago, Martha walked out on Jameson for one of his closest friends. Even so, Martha senses a tone in Jameson's voice that makes her realize he would auction-off his sole means of survival; his restaurant for her love again. Martha silently asks herself. "How could Jameson still care after what I did?" As she seeks after a sign of proof somewhere in Jameson's words after their call. As Martha's mind recollects how fast her heart was racing, she starts to search deeper. Martha imagined this goofy grin spread across Jameson's face as she smiles. *I could almost see it going from ear-to-ear as he answered the phone saying. Yes! You know this is Glen's favorite spot where he wines and dines all his ladies.*

As Jameson's words plays thru Martha's mind, she is more baffled than ever whether Jameson still loved her. Nevertheless; love or not, Martha was terrified Jameson would reveal these fifteen-year-old secrets; she has tried so hard to lay to rest.

Jameson stands before Martha all google-eyed, while Martha sits afore Jameson wearing this buried secret on her stunned face. Thomas notices Martha and Jameson, he removes a crystal flute from Jameson's hand. Raising the bottle of champagne up, Thomas fills Martha's glass for her. Since Thomas could plainly see Jameson wasn't willing or able to pour this lady's glass of bubbly or was the woman to receive it from him.

Before Thomas returns their champagne back to the ice bucket, he sits Martha's glass down before her, as he gaze in Martha's path, inquiring. "Are you sure I cannot satisfy you with one of our sandwiches?"

Martha replies as she lifts up her flute, "Darling, why would you even suggest one of your sandwiches when I desire your delectable seafood dinner pleaser!"

Thomas pretends to smile as he considers to himself about Martha. *She is one testing and challenging woman on the man's nerves.* Quickly, he gets through Martha's insults as Thomas asks Glen and Kali if he can refresh their drink for them. Glen smiles, assuring him they were okay and done with their dinner. Thomas promptly picks up their plates as Thomas says. "Good-night!" Then he wanders back to the kitchen to get a quick timeout from Martha, and her annoying ways. Thomas was convinced she was sent there to mess with his last minutes of the evening.

Suddenly Martha notices Jameson still standing there ogling directly into her face as he asks. "Well, hello sexy and how are you this spectacular evening?"

Martha restlessly sits trying to think of some way for her to exclude the suspicion Jameson's words cast upon them. Martha's begging eyes go skyward into Jameson's craving eyes as she fervidly asks. "And, what name shall I call you handsome fellow?" As she sits hoping for this all to go in her favor, and Jameson could pretend not to know her. Martha gasps nervously while Jameson winks voicing. "Hello, beautiful lady, I'm Jameson Milo! Now, what name would you be using tonight?" As he was not sure of what fictitious name game Martha's playing with Glen. But Jameson's willing to do whatever necessary at a chance to taste Martha's sweet lips again; even deceive his best friend, Glen, again.

Martha fumbles thru this notion of changing niceties with Jameson. Martha's heart quickly understands she is still in love with Jameson. Martha realized the one favor from Jameson to find Glen and Kali might be costly for her soul. Although Martha would never admit her truth. Martha was too afraid what if Kali finds out she already knew Glen all these years? Nevertheless, she'll just keep telling white lies to Kali, and her other snobbish friends to avoid unveiling her love for Jameson; it's too painful. Besides, how could Jameson ever feel the same way for Martha after the years of hurt she caused him and Glen. Whether Jameson wanted Martha or not, he still prowls around the table in Martha's presence with the begging, puppy dog eyes on her.

Observing the strange interactions between Jameson and Martha, Glen seems somewhat baffled as he stands up. He takes the chair from the adjacent table, gliding it closer to Kali. Sitting beside Kali, he leans over uttering in her right ear. "Kali, can you tell me what's happening here?" Kali shrugs her shoulder as he goes on. "What is supposed to be that romantic dinner for just two seems to be turning into an unasked-for foursome." As Glen's head rapidly leaps into defense mode. *My ladies usually do call me many things, but never a freak! I am strictly a one woman at a season kind of guy. And, whatever Kali and Martha have in their little games tonight, it's not what I signed up for. Absolutely not a part of any plans which my joystick desires to participate.*

Kali sees such despair written over Glen's handsome face as her heart is just as let down. She rotates to Glen, as he sits wordlessly alongside her. Kali tries to reassure him that Martha will not be staying long. Kali frowns at Martha hoping she'll get the message without her saying a word, but that is apparently not the case. Kali mouths off. "That little foolishness you have going on here, it is just not working tonight for Glen or me, Martha!"

Martha coyly grins. "Darling, I'm simply amazed you would even say such a thing about your dearest friend!"

Martha combs Glen's face as she ridiculously insists. "Beloved, and I thought it was so kind of you and Glen to request for little ole me to join you two tonight!"

Kali frowns as she asks Martha, "What gave you that crazy notion to believe either of us invited you!"

Martha sadly counters, "Sweetie, the champagne was the only invitation I needed." She pours a bit, inquiring, "Why otherwise would I send my dinner date home?"

Kali cuttingly counters, "Perhaps, you might want to go see if your dinner date is still around. Because we are certainly not the, who came to dinner replacement!"

Glen's head is swimming, as he sits there listening to

Martha go on-and-on dishing out such crap. Even if his silence might be golden, Glen is stressed. He recognizes all of Martha's havoc is messing with his romantic plans with Kali. Most of all, his own game plan, and Glen has had enough. He pipes up, irritably saying. "Martha, that little soiree you believed is going on here, just ended!"

Looking away from Martha, Glen turns his attention back to Kali. He stares at Kali with such apologetic eyes before lastly letting Martha know that her company was not part of Kali or his after-dinner plans.

Gazing across the table at Martha, he retorts. "Kali's putting on her dancing shoes and she and I are going to continue our romantic time. A snapshot which has only room for two, Glen and Kali. Likewise, I'm positive the starry-eyed looking fellow, who stands beside you needs to get back to work. He does have a restaurant to run!"

As Glen fires Jameson the evil eyes, so he could quit gawking into Martha's face and return to work. Perhaps with Jameson gone, Martha would leave as well without all of the head-in-the-cloud attention she's lapping-up.

Kali's eyes glimmer as she leers into Glen's fiery eyes and uttering breathlessly. "Wow, a man in charge!"

Jameson takes Glen's advice as he gawps in Martha's face saying. "Forgive me for staring, but you look much like a woman I use to know in a past life." Gazing away from Martha, he looks at Glen asserting. "Sorry to spoil your evening. The least I can do is pick up your check!" Then Jameson swiftly walks away before Glen could get a chance to oppose him picking up their tab or view the shame which should have covered Martha's pretty face.

After Jameson rushes away, Martha sneers into Glen and Kali's path, sadly stating, "Well, I can see this costly champagne nor myself is appreciated here tonight. And, to think your friend was doing you, Kali, a huge favor!"

Kali inhales asking, "Martha, what on earth have you been smoking? Because the way I perceive the scenario, there is no favoritism in being an uninvited friend?"

Martha leers at Kali showing a bit of uneasiness, and disconnect with Kali, as she asserts. "Darling, it has not been easy for me to track you down until I thought of a dear old friend who let it slip out that you were here."

Kali heatedly asks. "And, what friend was this?"

Overlooking Kali's question, Martha heavily sighs as she conceitedly states. "And, when I think back over all the agony, I went thru to get this friend to spill his guts. I almost had to give away my fortune to find you."

Martha knows now, as she goes over the enactments inside her head, she could not bear to do nothing. How would Martha let Kali's heart get crushed by Glen while she just keeps quiet? On the other hand, Martha knows to tell Kali the truth; after so many years, Martha would lose this respect she has earned over the years. Also, for Martha to spill her guts about Glen, she must reveal her lengthy engagement to Jameson. An era in Martha's life, which she's not proud of and doesn't want to resurface. Also, Martha realizes that Kali would finally understand Glen was not this stranger who she made him out to be in her life. But sharing such secrets, after all these years, might cause Martha not only Kali's respect but the only real friend which she ever truly loved besides Jameson.

Kali is mystified by Martha's words, as well as, those uncanny games Martha has been playing all night. Kali's not for certain, but she believes Martha's envy is getting the best of her. And, it's Martha's way of reassuring her friends that Kali's date wasn't with Glen Monroe. Kali's mind believes she has it all figured out. But in all reality, Kali didn't have a clue, as her soul slowly feels an ounce of guilt from Martha while Kali says. "Martha, I will not need that nudging you do so well or you to jump in and run interference." Kali ogles at him thru passionate eyes while serenely voicing to Martha. "I now realize Glen is a man of a few lyrics. However, every mouth full he has spoken, it has been for me. For him, tonight is all about my happiness. And, there's one more thing which could make tonight better, and that's you not being here!"

In Kali's mind, she sees Glen as this caring man. For Kali, a man who steps up, and defends a woman like he did must desire the woman, not her money. Even so, all she wishes for was just one night of adventure with him with no strings attached. A night Kali deserves after the many years she had spent pining away for Glen!

"Well!" Martha sighs, as she huffs. "Why did I waste my precious time traveling, all the way across town, just to be humiliated by you!" Faking tears, Martha goes on, "We all must leave at some point, and that's my cue!"

Kali opens her mouth to speak, as Martha throws up the hand preventing Kali. In a hurry, Martha pushes her chair away from their table. Martha stands up and grabs hold of the bottle of champagne. She observes Kali and Glen's cloned expression on their face as she unhappily utters. "Beloved, a person can tell when her company is not needed or wanted! So, I'm leaving; enjoy the rest of your evening! And, Kali, please ring me tomorrow."

Approaching the front door, Martha realizes, she did not have a ride home. She spirals about hoping Glen or Kali might feel sorry for her when Martha's melancholy eyes bond with Jameson's enthralling pair of eyes.

Jameson rapidly rushes to Martha's support. He asks her curiously, "Martha, why are you so upset? Did Glen or Kali says something to run you away?"

Martha flickers her sexy eyelashes as she bites on her lower lip tearfully uttering. "Yes, there's just no room at their table for three." Martha wipes her eyes as she goes on. "And, after my being so amiable to them both, I am left without a ride home."

Jameson's being allured into Martha's games again as he avidly glares into her eyes, uttering. "Please allow me to take you home!"

Martha smiles. "Darling, you are too kind!" While all the time she knows without the fake tears, Jameson will drive her home. Yet, what she's not ready for is his next shocking verses to her ears as he queries. "Martha, after fifteen years of me missing you, I am flabbergasted that you only called to ask me about another man, not even, me! Especially, Martha, since I have been avidly waiting for your call for over fifteen years!"

Martha realizes Jameson deserves an answer, but she has none. She stands glaring into Jameson's willing eyes knowing he was such a good man. As Jameson was this man, who gave her a home when Martha was penniless. These high-class get-togethers didn't exist, and Jameson was a friend, who nestled Martha's hand thru her trying times. Even so, Martha's new lifestyle of bougie friends mixed with cheating afternoon tea parties didn't leave a place for Jameson; not a working-class man.

Glen stands waiting for Kali to get-up as he stares at Jameson slither his arm around Martha's waistline. Glen thinks it is peculiar for Jameson to be escorting Martha; especially when they were strangers. However, Jameson and Martha has been performing weird; especially, after Jameson brought Martha's glass to the table.

Although; strolling out of the door smiling, Jameson and Martha were quite chummier than strangers. Mixed up over it all, Glen asks Kali to determine if she noticed the same. As Kali's friend, Martha grips onto Jameson's arm and cavorts cross the threshold proudly laughing.

Chapter Nine

Abruptly, Glen asks Kali. "Did you see a connection between our friends; Jameson and Martha?"

She grins, saying. "Well, it's funny you, and I noticed the same oddness in our friends. Particularly, when they both were make-believing not to know one another."

"Yes!" Glen hastily barks as he asks himself. "Why?" As his brain slowly starts to connect these missing dots, Glen gets panicky. Mostly, because the memory ripping thru his mind was of a woman who Glen doesn't desire to remember. As he tries to block the woman out of his thoughts, Glen's eyes displays such an emptiness.

Once they were outside, Glen affectionately rests his arm around Kali's shoulders. He smiles, avidly uttering. "With all your loveliness before these eyes of mine how can I let such a trivial matter take the presence of you!"

Kali returns his smile without stating a word as Glen escorts her to the car. Leisurely walking by his side, Kali glowers skyward into a sea of questioning eyes. As Glen was praying for the woman, Martha Hayward, not to be the same one he once knew.

Opening the car door, Kali noiselessly takes her seat. As he closed Kali's door, Glen's head starts to backslide into his past. His mind rapidly voyages thru these years.

Glen finds it harder to shake this picture of Jameson and Martha embedded in his brain. Also, the last words, his ears overheard from Jameson to Martha which were slightly melancholy as Jameson uttered to Martha. "You look much like a woman I use to know in a past life."

Suddenly, stepping around the car, Glen starts to see openly the bond which Martha, Jameson, and he shared together. It was during the year Jameson first purchased the SeaShore's Steak and Seafood restaurant. It was just another phase during Glen's prime years of life, yet why would he forget such dreaded memories of Martha?

Glen's body starts to perspire. He is overwhelmed as he vigorously sucks in a huge gulp of air while stopping in his tracks. Glen breathlessly questions himself. "Why was Martha playing these trifling games of make-believe and pretending she didn't know me? Was it for my sake or Kali's sake? After all these years, is Martha still trying to ruin my life again with her scheming and lying?"

Even so, without proof, Glen isn't about to mess up his romantic mood with Kali. Glen didn't find any need to tell Kali anything about Martha's or his past for now, as he continues to the driver's side of the car.

Opening his door, Glen's eyes eagerly looks in Kali's face wondering if she already knows the secret. As Glen situates himself within the car seat, he ardently inquires. "Didn't I promise you a night of dancing pretty lady?"

Kali fires a sexy smile saying. "I believe you made an allusion to dancing in the air for the two of us tonight."

Glen arousingly laughs, as he asks. "Is there a special place you'd like to go? If not, I have in mind a jazz club that I believe you might like!"

Kali grins as she gazes in his handsome face. "I'm all yours tonight. And so, your aspirations are there for me to make them all come true!" Hearing the rhymes aloud Kali's core realizes she is tired of searching for the whys of her life. When Kali only sought after her reasons not to turn Glen's heart away from her. The man Kali loves and whose soul her roots are starting to sprout within.

Over the years, Kali knew her feelings were stronger than her lustful sexual cravings for Glen. However, Kali never anticipated love. How's it possible for her to love such a man as Glen? Perhaps she's mistaking her fleshly desires of hers for so much more? Kali's irrational heart of hers just frolicked an extra beat from a bed of lust to love; the impossible. Nonetheless, Kali's soul has falling utterly in love with a store-bought man, Glen.

Kali delves into her brain to understand how or why she's allowing her heart to want Glen. A man, who Kali vowed to never give more than her money and time for soothing a bit of her nightly licentious pleasures. A little loving from Glen was only suppose to replace the thirst Kali had for Joseph's in her bed. But, now seated across from Glen, Kali's core wanted his love more than sex.

As she sits craving Glen, Kali could sense from such a desirous look in his eyes, he wanted her, too.

Then, she hears Glen fervidly affirms. "Kali, you are

such a desirable woman. In fact, I have never wanted or met any woman which I have craved more."

His mind glanced back a second to ponder the crazy day when he and Kali first met. In his heart, it appeared like weeks ago, when it was only yesterday. He thinks to himself that it's such a short time as Glen moans within to mitigate a debilitating hunger for Kali. A thirst that is so biting, it trounces away at him. Glen wouldn't permit such an emotion to surface; not now. Mainly, when this date is only supposed to woo Kali into playing his game of twisted love. And, for Glen, it only entailed the night filled with a romantic dinner for Kali and a few seconds of passion for him. Glen looks in Kali's face whispering to himself. "Not love! It can't be as this was just not the way our date was supposed to transpire!"

Starting up the engine, Glen rapidly pushes the knob to silence this loud music playing on the cassette player. Glen's a bit stressed. He wants some peace-and-quiet to sort out the strange happenings of a crazy heart. At that same time, Kali's happy Glen turned the sound off. She needs a quiet moment to understand what was going on as Glen barge in on her thoughts asking. "Did you want to listen to the music?"

Kali softly utters. "I'm actually enjoying the quiet."

Glen laughs. "Well, it is only a twenty-minute ride to where we are going, so enjoy it while you can."

Kali and Glen both rides along intensely sorting thru the underlying moments of their date so far. When Kali glances over at Glen smiling while thinking. *Can I survive a twenty-minute drive hungrily craving Glen when I see in his eyes that I am his desire; even if his eyes were fixated on the road.*

As she sits near Glen with passionate thoughts going throughout her core, she avidly hears him saying. "Kali, it's time to discuss us. Where it's going or just what this thing might be between you and me."

Kali starts to probe through her brain for the answer to Glen's questions. She does a little soul examining for herself to determine whether this was about his appetite for her. Kali begins to wonder. *Was Glen's essence suddenly revisiting his feelings for me? Or maybe some new scheme of his to get closer to the hidden treasures beneath the covered red lacey veil!*

Shaking her thoughts free of these uninvited notions of hers. Kali lightly sighs before asking. "Glen, what are your expectations for us?"

Glen replies, "Honestly, I'm not sure, but I know it's a discussion you would like to have at some point. I am thinking sooner, rather than, later will work for me."

First of all, it was so unexpected of Glen's tongue to be so outright about his affections for any woman. This was not an indispensable criterion for a stopgap man as Glen. Not, when he wants a woman to be short-lived in his life. But, his desires for Kali were something special. Glen's passion for Kali makes the simple word from his lips take on a sweltering hunger for her love.

His core demanded a different connection with Kali, which was so strange for him. As suddenly Glen's heart is craving a woman's love verses his intriguing game for revenge filled with lust and heartbreak he always plays.

Glen's soul is unexpectedly sensing something about

Kali which soothes the essence of his core by just being near her. This was an emotion so unfamiliar to his heart as Glen inhales a gulp of air while casting a long stare at Kali. Glen's mind was so topsy-turvy he wasn't thinking clearly as he caringly asks within. "The love of a woman or is it a wondrous taste for a twisted shade of green?"

Glen didn't even know why he is tormenting his self in the first place. Mainly, when his preferred choice was always his warped game of love! However tonight, Glen is just a little offbeat; for the heart appears to crave Kali without any trickery or deceit. Needless to say, his heart is permanently struggling with these sudden affections.

Instead of games, for once, Glen opts for a woman's love. Glen recognizes he desires Kali's love as he brings his car to a stop before Sonnie's Lounge and Jazz Club.

Ardently glaring into Kali's face, he utters. "Well, get ready to dance this night away because we are here!"

Staring at the mass of people which were lined-up to enter this club, Kali looks at Glen asking. "Are you sure this is the right place because how will we all fit inside?"

Glen softly smiles, saying. "Kali, no need for worries because I'm in good with the club owner."

Kali smiles saying. "Who are you not friends with?"

Ignoring her crack, Glen excitedly voices. "Oh, I am sure you will enjoy these jazz singer impersonators. The voices are amazing; so like the original performers."

Glen leers down at her wickedly smiling as he slickly glides his arm about Kali's waistline. Together, Kali and Glen sashays off to join the long lines of people talking, and waiting for the club doors to open.

Closer to the crowds, Glen takes hold of Kali's hand leading her pass the line of jolly faces; who seems to say hello. Glen boastfully walks up front to the entry doors.

Kali scowls up in Glen's face as she affirms. "You're going to get us killed here cutting lines in this crowd!"

Glen just smiles as a well-dressed, and ebullient man quickly removes this red cord from across the doorway. The man nods his head displaying a fun-loving smile, as he ushers Glen forward, voicing. "Good evening, Sir!"

As Glen fervidly lays his arm about Kali's shoulders, he and Kali stroll in harmony thru the door. It seems to Kali that all eyes in this club are ogling at Glen and her; a perfect couple. The belonging sensation, Kali's waited forever to feel by the side of a man. Overcome by these emotions, Kali's knees begins to shutter as the palms of her hands become somewhat moist. Kali rotates, gazing into Glen's eyes as she flirtatiously winks at him stating. "Someone forgot to mentioned their club VIP status!"

Glen boastfully snickers as he winks averring, "Well, what can I say, some of us just got it like that!"

Glen passionately stares in Kali's inviting eyes as she notices an appealing melody suddenly ends that plays in the background. Then, Kali inquisitively watches as this striking young lady, who somewhat portrays the spitting image to Etta James takes the stage. The woman casts a dazzling smile, saying "Please clear the floor. We have a special request this evening for an extraordinary lady!"

Kali's ears listen fixedly for the name of that woman as the band starts to play an arrangement that is familiar to her.

As this woman bellows out Kali's favorite song, "At Last", and the lights in the club go just slightly dim.

Kali cogitates within whoever that lady might be she is quite a blessed girl. Because for a man to devote such a song as wonderful as that one to her, then he, himself must be sensational or hopelessly in love.

Kali stands beside Glen wishing the woman was her. Glen avidly looks at Kali, as he affectionately takes hold of her hands breathing. "Kali, a little bird told me this is one of your favorite songs, so, may I have this dance?"

Kali is speechless as she glances heavenward into the beguiling eyes of a man who just took her breath away.

As a drop of moisture fills the corners of Kali's eyes, she seductively respires, "Well, I never anticipated to be the lady asked, yet I wished for it to be me!"

Glen fires a sexy wink into Kali's path as he ardently draws her nearer to him. Holding Kali in his arms, Glen knows this is the start of something more than his heart could ever perceive or wanted to as he inhales. "I could not have envision a more perfect passage tonight. Then being here; on this romantic dance floor, with any other woman than you, Kali Mathias!"

Kali's heart is pounding from the words which easily overflow from Glen's lips. In Kali's essence, he was not a man who will succumb to a feeling as prisoning to his heart as the love of a woman. Yet, was Kali perceiving a humane side of Glen Monroe? An affectionate side that he conceals from his women, so it consciously does not get in the way during his game of engaging their hearts.

As the entrancing voice of the woman begins to sing the lines. "I found a dream that I can speak to. A dream that I can call my own." Glen fervently gazes down into Kali's face zealously whispering. "I believe I have found this dream in you!"

Kali sees Glen's lips were moving, yet she has a hard time believing these melodious lyrics were flowing from his mouth. For Kali, this was unimaginable! What Kali's essence is hearing with every note of Glen's tongue was an airy melody of love. A stanza that seems to blow her mind away. Kali's eyes gaze skyward into a satisfied pair of spellbinding eyes which draws out such a charismatic smile from her lips. She utters, "Glen, and I have found the same in you!" Still gazing into Glen's face, he avidly smiles back without speaking a word.

Returning his passionate smile, Kali gradually lowers her head and softly rest it on Glen's chest. He embraces Kali closer within his arms as they continue dancing. At that precise moment, Kali's brain is wishing for a life of passionate dances in Glen's arms. However, Kali knows such a bond isn't conceivable with a store-bought man.

Chapter Ten

*A*lthough she couldn't have the man, Kali wishes for a taste of his sweet lips at this instance. One ardent kiss, which will set both their souls on fire for each other.

Amazingly, it's as if Glen was reading Kali's thought. Glen affectionately strokes her left cheek. Then, folding his hand, Glen tenderly places it under Kali's chin. Glen softly tilts her face upward. Searching out Kali's mouth, he heatedly puts his lips on hers, eagerly kissing them.

Although she is a bit staggered, Kali willingly returns Glen's steamy caress back. A heartfelt kiss so untainted, yet so arousing it makes Kali's lips desire more. As Kali amorously seek Glen's mouth setting his lips aflame.

Glen and Kali's hearts were suddenly moving in that perilous zone called love. A place in their life where her heart wants to go, but his heart is still trying to fight the challenge. Glen's mind couldn't understand what a man of his caliber would do with the love of a woman. Right then, Glen's brain reminds him again that he would not be able to have both Kali and his reprisal.

It's a difficult choice since he had never known such passion for any woman as he does Kali. And, Glen likes the fervent emotion that runs thru his veins from Kali's caress. A sensation so earth-shattering, it's making Glen forget about his selfish ways for a bit more of her lips.

On the other hand, these strong emotions he felt for Kali is setting Glen's core ablaze bit-by-bit. Kali's adore is taking Glen's soul by storm as he whispers to himself asking. "Has my foolish heart finally discovered the one woman whose love I crave more than my own?"

Glen's thinker wasn't transmitting the wrong signals. For once in Glen's entire life he was in love. He realizes now that the love of a woman means more to him than any sort-after retribution. Well, at least Kali's love does.

For Kali's love, Glen is suddenly willing to get rid of his name off the player's auction block to exclusively be only hers. Glen has such an awkward time as he tries to understand the emotions of his heart. His puzzled mind doesn't recognize where the foolish heart was conjuring up this love portion as he tries to force a smile for Kali.

Glancing up into Glen's face Kali could see his mind racing a mile a minute, but just assumed it was the mess among Jameson and Martha. A matter she would rather not partake of, not when Kali is having such a romantic night with Glen. And, what a joyful moment for Kali as she sees Glen; an unwilling man, increasingly revolve to her full-time lover. That special place in her heart where Kali has hungered for Glen to take over since Joseph.

However, when these romantic verses of Etta James ended. So, did Glen's intense moments of desires in the making for Kali seems to fade within the midair.

Glen's past heartbreak wasn't ready for the emotions

which came with this fiery touch of Kali's body dancing so close to his. It was an anxiety so familiar to his heart, Glen was afraid. Yet, at the same time, he wants to hold on and not let go of Kali or the sweet taste of her love.

Mystified, Glen deeply sighs! As he slowly bit-by-bit, unwraps his arms from around Kali's waist. Watchfully, he notices Kali's face as he dolefully asks. "Kali, do you mind if we leave now?" As Glen moves apart from her, Kali emotionally respires softly as she asks. "Glen, I am a little bit bewildered. So, what happen to that romantic night of dancing you promised me?"

Glen exhales as his facial mood take on a worrisome look. "It's been a long night for me, and I am worn-out so if you don't mind." He inhales softly. "Let's just go!"

Glen knows to tell Kali the real reason they must go, he must share his past heartbreak. And, Glen's core was not ready to go there. Even if, his essence is developing such a sweltering appetite for Kali.

As Glen looks away from Kali, he scuffles within to conceal that feeling. But, how could he, when the mere scent of Kali's perfume mixed with her velvety skin was driving him insane? His soul realizes Glen's too weak to survive one more dance, cheek-to-cheek, under such an impractical setting. If so, he knew it could yoke his core to Kali's forever. A final step, which Glen isn't ready to take with Kali yet, as he overheard Kali's disappointing, soft voice stating. "I am here with you. So, I am at your beck and call or did you forget that!"

Unfortunately, Glen couldn't see the humor in Kali's statement as he slightly frowns replying. "Just a warning but your chauffeur is about to leave now."

Sad, Kali hastily walks out of the door ahead of him. Glen knows he isn't physically tired, but emotionally his body is drained. Glen is exhausted as the voice inside of him desired satisfaction over love. A battle that the soul was getting too weary to ward off tonight.

Nearing the car, Kali suddenly pauses as she steps to the front of Glen taking his hands within hers. Kali was not sure what is wrong. But she knows Glen was acting a bit strange. Not at all like that man who picked her up tonight. Kali stares within this downhearted face asking. "Is there something which you care to share with me?"

Glen dimly smiles as he speedily replies, "Well, there are a few things we need to discuss."

Kali's face turns serious as she utters. "I am all ears."

Glen lovingly releases his hand from within Kali's as he avidly lays his hands on her shoulders. He turns Kali to face forward saying. "The discussion would be better in the car while we are seated." Glen caringly takes hold of Kali's left hand leading her to the car in silence.

She could not imagine what he has to say, which was so severe that they must be seated to continue. In Kali's heart, she has such a sinking feeling. It is as if they were going to open that locked seal to Pandora's box soon as they reach Glen's car.

Glen's face appears sad as he opens the car door. He hungrily stares into her eyes while Kali promptly takes a seat in the car. Closing her car door, he gradually circles about the vehicle to his driver's side. Anxious, Glen ajar the door while inhaling deeply before getting inside. He adjusts himself in the seat, then faces Kali and takes her by the hands. "Frankly, I am not sure where to begin?"

Kali's heart didn't want to fathom what would come next. In her mind, nothing could possibly make her feel worst than ending their romantic evening of dancing.

Kali removes her hands from Glen's hands. So, with a heart full of despair, Kali passionately fixes a hand on the side of Glen's face. As she softly rotates Glen's face within her eyesight. Kali devotedly leers into his eyes, as she expresses. "Out with it! Because whatever it is I'm a big girl, and my sad heart can take it."

Kali exhales a large gulp of air to get herself ready to hear whatever Glen has to say. Even if, his words might not be what her heart desires to withhold as Glen edgily starts to say. "Okay!" Suddenly, Glen's voice declines to a milder tenor as he goes on. "Well, first of all, I am not sure why Martha was playing games with us, tonight!"

Kali stops Glen, curiously asking. "How so?"

He starts again. "Cutting thru the games, I've known your friend Martha for over fifteen years." Suddenly, he sees a look of shock cover Kali's face as he quickly goes on. "Although; both she nor I have seen one another in years, and I suppose we've grown-up. So, I truly did not recognize Martha."

Kali inquisitively asserts, "How would anyone forget a woman as beautiful as Martha?"

Glen reservedly says. "Well, with Martha it wasn't an easy task!" For a split moment, Glen reconfigures in his mind just how cruel Martha treated his friend, Jameson. Although he didn't know the new Martha. But the lady, he and Jameson, once knew years ago was so worth not remembering in Glen's mind. And, he couldn't envision Jameson or anyone, not feeling the same about Martha.

Kali softly asks. "Were you two ever a couple?"

Glen mildly laughs, averring. "No, never anything of the sort, but that's Martha's story to tell of how she met Jameson and me."

Kali frowns at him puzzled. "Oh, so Jameson knows Martha too!" She slightly laughs. "So many surprises."

Glen frowns. "Yes! I suppose it was that strangeness I felt seeing Jameson and Martha acting more like a pair of lovers than strangers which bothered me."

Kali marvels at him asking, 'Why was that so bizarre; after all, Martha is irresistibly attractive to most men?"

"I would rather not say," as Glen's head muses for a few seconds before going on. "But that is when this old brain became a bit curious about Martha with her trivial out-of-the-way messages she kept dropping at dinner."

Although, Kali might not see that big picture of why Glen was letting the ordeal among Jameson and Martha send his night so topsy-turvy. At the same time, she is a bit perturbed Glen didn't find a need to share the truths sooner with her. What else was Glen keeping from her?

Kali's curious face turns into a frown; she glowers at him asking. "Why did you wait so long to tell me?"

Glen guardedly begs. "I truly did not remember who Martha was. At least, not before, I was getting in my car for the drive here. So, why spoil our romantic dance?"

Kali's eyebrows pucker as she ogles at him asking. "I see! Yet, that doesn't account for the question, why?"

"Honestly, Kali, I did not know how to tell you." He

gawps at her with regretful eyes. "Then again, I thought such news might interrupt our romantic evening!"

Kali looks away from him asserting. "Didn't I have a say-so in whether this evening should continue?"

He answers. "Yes, and I am sorry if I took that away from you," as Glen considers. *What difference would it had made telling Kali before now? In any case, I could not see spoiling a date, which was going much better than either me or Kali would ever have imagined tonight. Selfish or not I am feeling bad for not telling her.* Glen regretfully sighs, stating. "I'm truly sorry Kali as I clearly didn't think my decision thru."

Although; Kali could hear the apology on Glen's lips along with the shameful look on his face, Kali was hurt.

Kali asserts, "For once, the sad, apologetic eyes does not work for me. I should have been part of this choice which affects me, too. Notably, when Martha's a friend to me; and apparently yours, as well."

Glen's not sure how to react to Kali's words. As this woman; he once knew, was never anyone's friend other than Martha's. And, from Martha's same demeanors, he didn't understand why she wasn't recognizable sooner.

Nevertheless, a simple apology was all he could offer Kali now as Glen switches on the engine and drives off. Then, clearing his throat, Glen states. "I admit mucking this up. Yet, at the time, not telling you seemed right."

"We both agree, you messed-up." Kali lightly laughs, "Still, I would like to know more about that situation of you knowing Martha for so long." A tale Kali could not see why Glen was not forthcoming with all the details.

Glen replies. "Kali, I would prefer it if we didn't talk about it any further; it's not my story to share as I said."

"Why!" Kali implores. "Just whose skeletons are you trying to hide, your's or Martha's?"

"Kali!" Glen declares. "Martha's business is her own to tell you whenever Martha wishes." Glen stays silent a brief moment to catch his breath and think. As his head quickly goes into a wondering mode. *Why is Kali acting so heartless right now? She's not at all like the passionate lady, who I picked up tonight for our date! Kali's beginning to perform more like I remembered her friend, Martha. Always wanted to demand Jameson's whereabouts while Martha tried to run his life for him. Although; Kali was right about one thing, I am trying to hide my own skeletons, yet Martha had a few of her own, too.*

Removing the notions from his mind, Glen goes on, "And, as for me, I would much rather allow our former lives to stay, just that, in the past."

She gazes at him stating. "Just know all the skeletons in our closets has a way of coming to the surface!"

Glen retorts. "You might be right! Yet one thing you are not grasping about me is that I am a very low-keyed man. And, the attention your style of life brings, I don't want or need in my life right now."

Utterly mystified, she questions. "What does such an idiotic statement like that even mean?"

"First of all Kali, for a man who enjoys his privacy, I am saying your lifestyle brings too much drama."

She asks. "Drama! Whose playing games?"

Glen leers straight at the road before him because to share his feelings with Kali was so difficult. Particularly, when he has a burning appetite that he couldn't fathom for her. Glen hopes Kali can grasp what he has to voice with poise and not get upset, he carries on. "Well, there is no easy way to say it, other than, you possess way too much personality for me!"

Shaken, Kali astonishingly asks. "What do you mean by too much personality! Well, that is a first because no man has ever characterized me as such before."

Glen sadly says. "Kali, I am only stating what I sense about you within my soul at this point in time!"

"Glen!" Kali says as her voice barely rises above this calm whisper, she carries on. "I thought when I became an adult I would lay aside my stupid games. However, I must confess getting you to take me on our date was an idiotic game to me; at first, but no longer."

Kali's heart is pounding rapidly, as she searches for a way to tell Glen her truths. How do you let a man, who she has lustfully desired for so long, know her irrational heart was suddenly in-love with him. Kali wasn't certain herself when these crazy desires went from lust to love.

Chapter Eleven

*K*ali envisions it was during the entrancing strains of her favorite song. Or, it might have been when Glen so passionately wrapped her in his fervid arms during their fiery kiss. Nonetheless, for Kali's core, it doesn't matter that exact time or place when her innocent soul decided to stop lusting for Glen's virility. Not, when Glen's soul sought after a bit of her assets rather than her core. But, for Glen, Kali understands what he required most is for her essence to grasp his secret language of love. Even if Kali's heart looked-for a small sample of that incredible passion she'd seen of his love; Glen's just not ready.

Glen's afraid to give into such incapacitating feelings but not Kali. Her heart is willing to love Glen at all cost as Kali ardently admits. "Glen, I ask forgiveness for any part my games played in turning your heart away from a true love like mine." As her words ended, Kali notices a change in Glen's feelings without him speaking a word.

Kali knows it time to put pride aside, she begs. "Can I get another chance? And, ask you to trust in your own heart enough to grasp my feelings for you are real!" She feverishly awaits Glen's reply for a chance to know him better, and for him to see her love without any games.

No matter what the verses were; which escape Kali's tongue, Glen's ears only heard the word game. A sound which echoed loud and clear thru the center of his soul. These words to Glen's ears appear so tawdry, and crude as his heart suddenly searches for a way free. A way out of Kali's warped spellbinding game which has signs of a heartbreak written all over it for both of them.

It was like Kali's speaking the same language as him, so Glen understood her schemes. Yet, the judging lyrics for Kali, they lay on the back of his throat. Since he was a man of quite a few tricks of his own; in fact, he would consider himself a master of most. Nevertheless, Glen's not about to give his love to a woman who plays games too. He thinks a few moments. *How could this foolish heart be so wrong about choosing to trust in Kali's love?*

Just as the thought finish running thru his head, Kali whispers. "Glen, please say something; anything. I have no right asking you to trust my heart, but I am!"

Momentarily, Glen removes his eyes off the highway for a quick gaze at Kali. When unexpectedly Glen's eyes behold this temptingly pretty woman sitting beside him.

Glen exhales noisily as his essence long for this lady, who sits beside him in red. But in his head, Glen knows he'd never be happy if he opts for a woman with games versus revenge.

Glen's feelings for her no longer needs him to chose between Kali or a measly reprisal; not when she's seized his heart. He cautiously states. "What else could my lips possibly say other than I believe my heart loves you."

Tearfully, Kali passionately asks. "Am I hearing your words accurately? Because it sounded a lot like love."

"Yes!" Glen avidly whispers. "Yet, at this same time, I sense you are just not the one to loan my heart out to. Kali, I just can't be hurt again by the love of a woman."

As usual Kali's mind was probably over thinking this matter with Glen as her mind recalls the word *loan*. Kali couldn't understand how anyone can loan their core for hire. Somewhat puzzled Kali calmly questions Glen. "Is this some secretive adoring game of your's called love?"

She scowls at Glen as he gives Kali an impression he didn't care. Glen suddenly glowers straight ahead at this dark road before him without no display of emotions.

She unsettling asks. "How does one loan a heart?"

Kali was so confused. Her mind couldn't understand why her and Glen's evening rimming with a blossoming passion went cold. Suddenly, something quite beautiful, it appeared to go helter-skelter in a blink of one's eye.

Glen did not have any clue how to respond to Kali's question. He realizes that his heart didn't want to be on loan not to Kali. But what his heart does know is that it will not be exposed to the unbearable agony of handing your heart to someone, who will return it damaged.

For Mr. Glen Monroe's heart had experienced agony from the hurt of a woman's love. Although it was many years ago, this odd feeling Glen has in his heart for Kali is similar, yet so different. Because for Kali, he has such a trusting sensation inside his spirit of faith to know she will desire him only. A detached place of Glen's core he never dreamed of giving to any woman ever again.

But why should these emotions even matter to Glen when Kali's heart isn't solely his? Because for Kali to be his, it comes with undeliverable requests for a walk thru an unjust past life of knowing Martha and Jameson. For him, it will not work. Mainly, when he has no intentions of baring his soul of previous existence with Kali or any other woman. And, if those factors were a part of Kali's condition for accepting his affection. Glen would rather keep on playing his Twisted Game Of Love. After all, it was something Glen is more familiar with than this new tell-all requirement love which exposes his buried past.

Suddenly, the air inside the car goes silent, as neither Glen nor Kali could find the right word to express their feelings. They both were at a loss for the lines of poetry to recite which could alter the thoughts of their minds.

As Glen drives in quiet, Kali sits next to him praying that he might give them a chance to explore whatever it was between them. Without any doubt, Kali knows this was love for her but for Glen she has her doubts. Kali's heart just desires a second chance to explore the hidden boundaries of Glen's essence for her. Since she tasted a sample of this love when Glen heatedly swept her up in his arms while they danced. Kali sensed the warm adore amidst them as he fervently embraced her. Kali starts to muse about it all when she recognizes what is presumed to be the thought in her mind ejaculate out. "What man organizes such a romantic date with a special song for a woman he doesn't care anything about?"

Glen hurriedly returns. "When did I say I didn't care about you? I do not believe those words came from my lips; not once tonight." He smiles saying. "In fact, I was thinking of making "At Last" our song!"

Kali's face is encircled with the look of mortification all over it, as she processes Glen's words to heart. "You must forgive these words which escape my lips, but I'm a bit puzzled why you would even consider making "At Last" our song?"

"Kali," Glen softly states. "Because it truly expresses the way I feel about you. But, whatever is eating away at your heart, you are welcome to discuss with me."

Still embarrassed, Kali expresses. "No need! Besides, I would rather hear about why you desired to make "At Last" our song. Because the mere sound of these words make a woman's heart skip a few beats!"

Glen rejoins, "Okay! Just remember I'm right here if you wish to discuss anything, relating to my feelings for you, or the situation between us, tonight." As the verses parts Glen's lips, Kali sees he omits any asking of clarity about Martha and or his past. It seems such topics were not negotiable if Kali wants "At Last" to be their song!

Kali glares at Glen through the corner of her left eye as Glen carefully parks his car in front of her house. All her dreams were finally ending, as Glen switches off the engine. She could no longer remain quiet, as Kali softly, sighs saying to him. "I realize we really don't know one, another. But I have been praying for just one night with you of passion for so many years; however, I prayed for a much happier outcome than this one."

At that moment, Glen's heart wants so much to give his love to Kali, but a small voice inside of him reminds Glen to *wait.* His mind might have overlooked what the scone of a woman's love was like but not his devastated heart. He had chosen that path with a woman years ago which twisted his world upside down and made him the man he was today; a wounded lover.

Unsure of himself, Glen gradually turns to face Kali, he woefully voices. "I just believe my heart will desire a little bit more time for coming to terms with all that has transpired within it tonight."

With a heart bursting with fear, Glen sits asking Kali for a bit more time when he recalls why he would never share his past. Suddenly, he is reminded that sharing his past life with Kali might have a bad outcome. But if she unveils on her own Glen's character as a dejected lover, it could be worst. Just the mention of the Seasonal Man might deter Kali's burning passions flowing deeply thru her veins for Glen.

A skeleton which Glen owns so sinister it would tear Kali's world apart from love. A secret Glen had no clue Kali already has heard so much about thru Springfield's local gossip. Mostly, Kali heard Glen desires his women with lots of money. Even if, Kali plays ignorant to what she has heard about Glen, her heart still requires to be a part of his misfit world of love.

Kali patiently sits listening to this melody oozing out from Glen's lips to her heart. She couldn't imagine why Glen would request more time from a heart that indeed adores him. Still, she smiles, stating. "Please, take all the time you desire. Though, keep in mind, my heart's been imprisoned by you so long, it can't wait much longer."

He rapidly replies, "Kali, I truly understand, but I do hope you give me a little more time to figure out what's transpiring inside my heart for you."

Kali glowers into Glen's pleading eyes knowing she's not going anywhere. Although; Kali's mind is still vague on the way to gain access to Glen's heart, she is staying.

Why would Kali leave the man who she has waited a lifetime to hear him fervently utter just her name in that same sentence with the word love? Kali realizes she's in love with Glen, but she also recognizes that he's in love with her. However, Glen's heart could not comprehend his feelings or too afraid to admit it to himself or her.

Glen wasn't Kali's first love, but she definitely wants him to be her last love. Suddenly, a man she lusted after for so long, she desires so much more with him. As she glances away from him a small tear forms at the edge of her eyes while Kali tearfully voices. "Only as long as my heart will allow me to wait for you!"

Hearing those lyrics from her lips, Glen's heart finds a bit of hope. Because Glen understands that blistering, raging sensations which intensely runs thru his soul was undoubtedly stronger than his raging testosterone. Glen realizes the fiery emotions just might be a physical thing among him and Kali. Specially, with all of Kali's sudden appeal enticing his eyes now. Though, what Glen's core is undertaking was so exhilarating to him. Like no other feelings Glen's essence has ever known for any woman.

He's even dreaming of a fairy-tale ending; something Glen never needed before. In Glen's eyes, this seems so much like love to him. Yet, a feeling his soul was scared to confess aloud to Kali as Glen voices. "I'm looking to receive the same confidence you're requesting from me. I am asking you to believe in me, and the deep affection inside my heart for Kali Mathias; so will you stay?"

Kali looks down as she avidly voices. "It's possible!"

Unexpectedly, Glen realizes he wishes to embrace all of his unknowns with Kali, than without her. He knows whether without or with fear, she would never abandon his side while he weathers the storm of love. Therefore, Glen grasps it was time to share his entire life with Kali.

He needs Kali to meet that man he was, and the new one he wants to be for her. Glen will share, not only his prior life but also this need for a woman's reprisal. How otherwise would Glen breathe these lyrics, I love you to Kali when he is not straightforward with himself or her. How can Glen plead for Kali's trust; a woman he loves, when he doesn't even trust himself?

Kali's heart desires so much to trust long-term in his veiled feelings for her. But her core is too afraid to take this risk. Right now, what Kali's spirit needed was some sort of assurance, not just Glen's avid verses of rhymes. Simple words which could waiver in the blink of Glen's eye and leave nothing but empty promises for her heart to hold on to. As Kali slightly drops her head to ponder her mind a minute such a thirst for Glen takes presence as she fervidly inquires. "Does your heart even trust me enough to stick around until you've figured it out?"

Glen stares into Kali's passionate eyes as he ardently indicates. "Until meeting you, Kali, my heart was always leaping from woman to woman. I had become so afraid to trust just one; nor did I care if they trusted me."

Kali caringly inquires, "What were you so afraid of?"

He breathes out a deep lungful of air before carrying on. "I suppose since I grew up in a do-unto-others time culture before they can-do-unto-you. In my world, trust didn't exist much; therefore, I never found any purpose in a meaningless emotion; not until meeting you."

Kali exhales loudly, requesting. "Glen, why me since I am sure there have been many women in your life?"

Glen avidly affirms, "There's something refreshingly unique about you that lets me believe I can trust in you; even when I don't trust myself."

"Glen," Kali gently echoes. "I am honored you have placed such high confidence in me. And, know, you can trust me with your heart always; so, will you?"

Chapter Twelve

"*T*rust!" Glen joyously laughs, "I realize in the past a woman's words hasn't been very trustworthy. However; with you, I desire not only to trust in you but learn how to give love the way you deserve it; unconditionally."

Even though Glen had a slight taste of love; still, his heart is unsure of how to express such a feeling when it is being returned. But, Glen does know when he's ready to devote his whole heart to Kali, it must be right. Glen realizes his heart desires Kali, but there is a small matter which requires his attention before he can give his heart to Kali. Mostly, because Jo-Ann Parks is still very much a part of his seasonal existence.

Glen knows he must break the news flash to Jo-Ann that her season has come to its crossroads with him. As of tonight, every inch of Glen's soul is in the custody of Kali. Not just for a season because with Kali, he desires a forever. As Glen knows only one season couldn't ever be long enough to quench his desires for Kali.

Glen never anticipated just one night with Kali; who wasn't even his type of woman, would turn into a world of looked-for tomorrows for him. Glen devotedly looks at

Kali as he utters within, "How was that even possible for me; she is not even my fancy?" As his eyes fervently glow within Kali's eyes, he flickers a sexy wink followed by a broad affectionate smile.

Suddenly, Kali notices a side of Glen that makes her believes she had a man who was becoming trustworthy. A man who wants to love her unconditionally. Her face radiates with passion, as Kali recalls Glen's breathtaking verses. Gazing into Glen's eyes, Kali breathlessly utters. "I believe your spoken phrase is the sweetest words any man has ever said to me, and truthfully meant it!"

Glen glances into Kali's face as he ardently expresses while recognizing he must clear his life of Jo-Ann. "For you, Kali Mathias, I desire to be a better man. The man, whose life is free of his present uncleared up baggage."

Kali is mesmerized by the fervid glow which spreads across Glen's handsome face as this melody escapes his lips. Had they finally crossed over the boundary lines of lustful voracity or retribution? Is Kali eventually taming her shrewd seasonal man to thirst for only her? Was his heart forgetting those other three seasons of the year?

In her heart, Kali can visibly see this new way Glen's eyes were suddenly beholding her. Before his vision sits an irresistible Kali who Glen's appetite wants to be near now. And not Kali, the undesirable woman, who Glen's eyes once avoided. It was like Glen is finally following a yellow brick road straight into the direction of her heart and soul. And, Kali's loving every bit of his attention!

Finally, this was the looked-for assurance Kali needs.

Her heart is content, she has found a lifetime of endless days in Glen; a store-bought man. Kali's soul is rivetted with Glen as she fervidly affirms. "Now that both of us have bared our souls to one another!" She slightly grins, asking. "Where will this bond of love go from here?"

Glen avidly replies. "Kali, I realize it's only been one night, but my heart does not want you to go anywhere."

With these fervid emotions brewing inside of Glen's heart, it would destroy him, if Kali walks away now. His essence is spellbound by Kali, but he recognizes it's not entirely his to give away to her. Since currently, whether he liked it or not, Glen's mixed-up emotions involve his current seasonal woman, Jo-Ann Parks.

Although; Glen's feelings were not close to the word love for Jo-Ann, they were still an item. Yet, with a new passion of desire for Kali, Glen hopes Jo-Ann would be somewhat understanding and let him out of the loveless bond in the mist of her season. Especially, since no hint of nothing close to love ever parted from either of their tongues during Jo-Ann's season.

As Glen sits staring into Kali's face; the only woman his heart could love, his soul begins to grieve. Suddenly, Glen's essence prays for some sort of reprieval from his loveless rapport of a relationship with Jo-Ann. Because; for him and Jo-Ann it was only lustful desires and Glen always knew. However; now finding Kali, he recognizes his heart could never love Jo-Ann. Not the way he truly loves Kali. At that instant, Glen knows he couldn't ever have this google-eyed sort of feeling for any woman but Kali. Because Kali's love was so different. It made Glen feel alive for the first time since his heartbreak. And, his essence feels a connection between him and Kali which was so mesmerizing it completes his whole soul.

Glen's body was aching to be set free from a woman he will never love so he can give his all to Kali. Because she's the one he truly wants; not Jo-Ann. How could he not ask to be free of such shenanigan after experiencing Kali's heart throbbing type of love? What a spellbinding sensation which has Glen's spirit awe-struck by the soft touch of her tender lips as he leans over kissing Kali!

As Kali and Glen's lips avidly parted, he sensed such a sweetness. A hunger so sweltering it heatedly takes his breath away with every mouthwatering, tasteful stroke.

What once appeared like a prison sentence to Glen's soul. His body suddenly requires it to even breathe; that love of a woman. A spirit which once starved to belong was now being spellbound by such an electrifying ardor of passion. For him, Kali's soul possesses a kind of love he must have. This alluring type of love which his heart never recognized exist until now. A thirstiness he's sure could never occur in his life with Jo-Ann nor within her existence for him.

Realizing that, Glen's confident Jo-Ann would never want to be a noose about his neck. How could she hold on to a man who doesn't or will never love her? Mainly, after he and Jo-Ann orally negotiated a contract of sorts before ever getting involved; no feelings attached. Also, Glen presaged Jo-Ann, he was just a seasonal man with no future plan for her or any woman.

Before Kali, Glen's heart only sought love to avenge

an essence scorched by what he thought was a woman's love. A woman who left Glen, just days before their big day of matrimony to marry the man of her own dreams, his beloved cousin. Even so, it was a woman, who Glen loved with all he had to give. A love which stripped him bare; only leaving a shell of a wounded, vengeful man.

Yet, with the sort of passion like Kali provides, Glen is discovering a new side of love. An awakening which's far beyond Glen's comprehension of what a future with any woman could ever be. Kali's fervor for Glen was so mind-boggling, it was almost impossible for his head to recognize. How could Glen's heart indeed be falling for Kali or any woman after such a heartbreak? Was Glen's feelings merely playing a devilish prank on him with the two women; a punishment perhaps? Although; not just any two women, Glen was intensely in love with one of them, Kali. Even if, Glen's time still belongs to Jo-Ann, his fervent heart will only have a place in it for Kali.

Glen knew when he asked Kali out on their date, his season with Jo-Ann was not over yet. Therefore, Glen's brainy scheme was to wine and dine, Kali, while he tries to score his next seasonal. However, Glen's essence did not realize it only took just one date for him to fall prey as a victim in his own twisted game. This master player, who has utterly fell in love with Kali; a prong within his own game. Suddenly, Glen recognizes, it was him, who got played by a force stronger than imaginable; love.

A stage where Glen's heart wasn't seeking to venture ever again as he fervidly peeks across within Kali's face. He realizes, his heart could not fathom Kali not being a pivotal part of such an unforgettable moment. But, also Glen's soul recognizes Jo-Ann might be offended.

Glen didn't intend to hurt Kali or Jo-Ann. Still, Glen realizes if emotions exist; whether love or not, someone might get hurt. Now, his heart breaks for both Kali and Jo-Ann. This new Glen could not imagine what kind of cruel man would permit these two ladies to undergo the brutality. As a tender voice within reminds Glen that he was the man. Just then, Glen's essence begins to twinge for all women; who was a seasonal, in his world of love, lust, and deceit; A Twisted Shade Of Green! A shade of coloring that a function of his brain does not recognize. He couldn't understand when the man afore him; in the car mirror, turned to be so cold-hearted as he questions himself. "Was this love?"

Glen couldn't realize why a word that once meant so much to his heart became so resentful for him. Even if, he was once dumped by what a woman professed to be true love for him. And, how could he allow an emotion to take him to such a shady place? A stage where a core can't grow passion into anything other than lust, love or deceit. An impossible age in Glen's life where affections could never exist; only torture. Mostly, Glen's scared of being consumed by this feeling which should have been so beautiful, but for Glen so ugly; love. That was a time in Glen's life where he trusted no one, not even God.

Glen's essence never truthfully sought for a way out; not until he danced with Kali. It was then his soul knew a taste of actual love. Glen realized soon as he fervently placed his arms softly around Kali's waistline, he felt an avid connection. An enthralling passion which bounded his heart to Kali's forever. This love magnified a feeling which's interestingly electrifying, yet still intriguing. Kali possesses an alluring aura which made Glen's soul want to take a second look at his dominant twisted conducts.

Suddenly, Glen's soul senses a weird feeling through and through his entire body as he begins to ache for the women. Placing his hands upon his lips, Glen whispers. "Lord, how can I seek forgiveness from all my seasonal sufferers that I have wronged?" As he prayed, Glen was trusting in God for a clean conscious for telling Jo-Ann the truth. Even if, he still sensed the hurt he had caused to so many women in his past. For Glen's soul, it seems unbearable for him to even picture, how he would want to play such a cruel game. Above all, not on Kali due to his own color stained soul inside.

Unexpectedly, Glen senses an intense impulse in the pit of his stomach. This urge to step up and say sorry to every woman he'd been so cruel toward. Mostly, to Kali and Jo-Ann, since they both appear to be part of his life during this same season. Glen recognizes because of his love for Kali, she needed to know all about him. That is the only way Glen knows to cleanse his soul, and at this same time seeks forgiveness of all the women and God.

Glen knows Kali's everything a man could want. But before he invites Kali into his heart, he must honor this verbal agreement between Jo-Ann and him. He believes Jo-Ann deserved; at most, that much homage from him before giving his whole heart to Kali. Even if, he knows Jo-Ann will never ever have a place in his heart nor him in hers; she still warrants the new Glen's respect. So, he wouldn't confess past or present woos with Kali before ending a season with Jo-Ann and receiving forgiveness.

All of a sudden, Glen finds himself becoming such a praying man as he starts sharing his thoughts with God. *Lord, help me to find peace within! Because I understand without forgiveness from You and Jo-Ann, how could I honestly commit to Kali or seek any type of clemency?*

It wasn't until just then, sitting across from Kali with a mind full of past regrets that Glen realizes such depth love brings. Not ever had a woman fulfilled Glen's soul with such joy before meeting Kali. A woman who Glen never meant to lose his heart to; tonight or anytime, yet this very moment, he was no longer afraid to love her!

Kali sits near him naive to it all as she never predicts Glen's facial frowns carried such havoc within his heart or even about another woman. She was clueless Jo-Ann owns a part of Glen's life or wedged among her and his happiness. Glen, that man who Kali has loved for most of her life. Therefore, Kali was ignorantly happy to hear the heartfelt words which escape Glen's sweet lips. Kali has no desire of ever leaving Glen; not when he's finally singing to the tunes of her heart. She truly believes a bit more time and Glen's core will know precisely what her heart has known for awhile. Glen's soul will discover an extraordinary love of a woman worthy of his trust. That one woman he has been waiting to believe in all his life.

Although Glen's craving wants to test Kali's treasure chest his heart could not. Suddenly, Glen fervidly stares into Kali's face stating to her, "Well, I hate to leave, but it is getting late. And, I believe we both have undergone quite a problematic night with affairs of the heart."

Right now, Glen's mind was focusing on solving this situation within his life. Glen begins to ponder just how he allowed himself to get into this two woman at a time debacle. *Why now heart? How can a heart fall so deeply for any woman after just one date? Kali was only presume to be Jo-Ann's successor; another seasonal.* Glen ominously shakes his head to remove an unsettling thought as he lovingly smiles at Kali. She returns an enticing grin with ideas of her own.

Kali's fiery appetite for him seems to overtakes all of her proper senses. As her treasure searches for a way to lure Glen's sexy body inside for one more sample of his sweet lips. Clearing her thirsty brain, Kali fervently asks. "Would you like to finish the conversation inside where we both can get a little bit cozier?" Quickly, Kali's heart starts racing as it hunger to feel Glen's body close.

Chapter Thirteen

Kali wasn't going to allow Glen and her date to have such a loveless ending. Kali's fiery lips couldn't let Glen go without one more taste of his sweet lips upon hers.

Tonight, Kali is ready to be tucked in bed along with all the thrills that comes with it. As Kali sits craving just a taste of Glen's passion, he is looking at her hungry for a chance to rock Kali to sleep all night long.

Even though Glen's manhood desired to be satisfied by the strokes of Kali's sugary kisses as his lips pleasure her treasure chest; he wouldn't. Since, in his mind, Glen feels to tuck her in bed tonight can be a somewhat risky mistake for both of them. A slip-up, Glen feels both he and Kali's erotic hearts might irrefutably live to regret if before his one-on-one with Jo-Ann. As he looks at Kali with eyes of uncertainty, Glen states. "Tonight, we both harbor so many wonderful thoughts within our heart of how tonight should end, or even be like."

Kali's brow fills with wrinkles as she avidly leers into Glen's eyes a bit lost, inquiring, "What do you mean?"

He caringly takes Kali's hands enfolding them within his hands as he asserts. "Perhaps, we should just call it a night and let all our sudden desires for one another take a cooling off period."

Kali is in disbelief to how any man would turn down a night of steamy lovemaking with a lady. Kali begins to doubt her own desirability. *Does Glen really desire me?*

Kali begins to search Glen's unsure face. As she was sure, her heart is not reading his lust for love all wrong.

She starts to look back on her and Glen's reasonably quirky events of their date. Kali believes she could have misunderstood her own sort after signal for Glen's love confusing it with her own lustful desires for him.

Kali removes her hands from within Glen's hands as her lips rapidly puckers around the edges. Kali requests. "Glen call me crazy or not, but am I the only one who's sensing this powerful connection brewing between us?"

Hearing the disappointment in her tone, Glen avidly expresses. "Oh Kali, if you can only sense these feelings which I have for you inside!" Glen lovingly glances into her eyes as he goes on. "The decision has nothing to do with you, it's me. Because I care so intensely, I desire to be able to give myself to you completely before we take our life of forever to that next level." Glen deeply sighs, "It's only right! Kali, you deserve the very best of me."

From their passionate dance to the fervent kiss, Kali believed she did have the very best of Glen. What more did Glen have to give her then himself right now? Since the man looking into Kali's face was all the masculinity, she desires. As a thirst starts to surface from within, she voices. "How will it get any better when the man I love, he does not want to savor the softness of my body next to his. Or this coolness of my breath as our lips meet in a fiery kiss." As soon as Kali's verses ended, Glen's face begins to frown as he avidly whispers. "I'm right here."

Kali lowers her eyes from staring into his eyes as she says. "I am not seeing him." As her core wants to know where is yesterday's Glen; the one who long to tuck her into bed as she tenderly asks. "What happen to the man with these raging hormones who craved me so less than thirteen hours ago that he had to tuck me in bed?"

Glen lightly laughs, as he asserts. "Kali, it seems that man might have grown-up within that time frame."

For once, Glen did love someone other than himself and did not want to taint it with any guilt or regrets. His heart respects Kali too much to make his move without first breaking it off with Jo-Ann. Before tonight, Glen's libido never turned down a night of a woman's passion. For Glen, it was only sex and the sweet taste of revenge it all delivered at his feet. It was strictly about the justice Glen always felt he deserved; never about love. But, for Kali, Glen's praying to become a better man and not an entrapper for any woman's twisted color of love again.

Glen knew unless he changed, a life with Kali wasn't likely conceivable for him. Even if, Glen had found the only woman who his heart desires a lifetime dream with since his heartbreak. Love has made Glen a new man!

Even so, Glen was having quite a challenging period recognizing Glen Monroe was the man, who sits before Kali was indeed him. But just the same, his core's liking that new Glen. A man, whose focus is suddenly soaring above a dark cloud of deceit. So, Glen knew his twisted games of fraud must die for him to be reborn to love!

Still considering Glen's last poetic lyrics in her mind, Kali notices such an enthusiastic glare on his handsome face as she heatedly breathes. "It is quite funny how our first date started with such an undefined romantic flare, yet ends with us desiring so much more."

Glen hurriedly comes back. "Funny! How so?"

Kali mildly replies, "Oh, it is a good kind of funny as we went from not knowing one another to a forever!"

Glen jokingly states. "Whoa! It appears we leaped up our ladder fast. Whatever happened to a slow beginning spot on the Monopoly board of life? Because it looks as if we never passed go, yet here we are at a forever!"

Kali somewhat laughs stating. "Oh, we passed go, so many years ago and neither of us even knew it!"

They both excitedly laugh as Kali's core suddenly no longer feels undesirable to Glen. As Kali admiringly sits leering into Glen's face, he softly breathes while stating.

"I know I asked for time to figure out these feelings but between the ride here and now things are a bit clearer."

Kali fires a sexy wink, voicing. "Nothing but love!"

Glen's core is overjoyed as he affirms, "Kali, I'm not sure what you did, yet you took my soul from a place of dubiety to one of promise without me even knowing."

Glen's heart was no longer in disarray about what he feels for Kali. But Glen still couldn't trust himself alone with Kali; not until he could commit solely to her. Glen gazes at Kali voicing. "I'm so glad we didn't allow more years to pass before I asked you on a date. If so, a heart would have been still lost while craving for the splendor of knowing such a passionate love of a woman."

Kali smiles with bliss as she gazes into his wondrous eyes filled with such adore, asking. "Would that woman just happen to be me, Mr. Monroe?"

"Kali, I never knew what it felt like to receive love in return." He laughs, declaring. "I've not known this type of happiness ever; not until you. In fact, I was lonely!"

Kali somewhat smiles, saying. "Now, I know you are just jerking my chain. Because how can a man that is as debonair as you be without whoever he chooses?

Without warning, Glen's facial look grows sincere as he gazes into Kali's face uttering. "Well, before meeting you, I lived a secluded life. And, at times, such a life can get a bit lonely. However, since meeting you, I sense it's about to change into nothing but sunshiny days."

Glen's quite the romanticist. Yet, Kali sensed it from the way he had fervidly swept her off her feet with such words from his tongue. She's overwhelmed by this kind man who sits across from her. Glen's more enchanting, lovable, and caring than she could have ever imagined a store-bought man to be.

Overcome with such desire for him, she passionately winks at Glen as she lovingly says, "When you're happy I am ecstatic because that is what caring for someone is all about; putting their feelings beyond yours!"

"Kali," Glen lovingly whispers as he takes her hands placing them within his hands embracing them lovingly. "Although you're a little complicated, I find the passion and your open-heartedness to love unbelievable."

As Kali's eyes observe that man, whose tongue these words were avidly flowing from into her ears. She could only trust that the man next to her was the right one for her heart. Even if, she had ached for that exact moment for what seems like a lifetime, now that it's before her it is a bit scary. However, terrifying this all was, it was that space in Glen's heart where Kali now senses he actually wants her to be. Never again would Kali's voice silently question her heart if Glen's love was real for her.

It was hard for Kali to choose the right words as she stumbles a little before enthusiastically expelling. "Glen, I've been longing and waiting for a precise moment like this with you that it doesn't seem real now." Kali lightly sighs before continuing. "It just doesn't appear real!"

Glen smiles uttering ardently. "Trust me, Kali, this is quite real. You're looking at a man who has found what true love really means tonight." He gently casts his eyes toward her breathing softly. "Not just love, but perhaps even that picture-perfect kind of love!"

This very second Kali's essence grasped her seasonal man is finally morphing into her forever man. Since this chase of Glen started, Kali had been brooding over him trying to figure out what could make a man with Glen's repute with the ladies choose her. Instantly, her essence no longer needs to wonder because this passion for her that Glen has was genuine. Passionately looking into his alluring eyes. Kali avidly props her elbow on the middle divider between their seat, as she fervently kisses Glen's lips over-and-over.

When Glen and Kali's lips softly separated, he avidly

stares into her waiting eyes. Glen realizes without her as the essence of his life, he couldn't survive past tonight.

He slowly exhales outward stating, "Kali, your kisses are so passionate and intense that I hunger to taste your juicy lips over-and-over again. And, I now recognize it's you; only you Kali, I desire every day of every year."

And, for Kali's ears to lastly overhear these romantic phrases from Glen's lips were quite flattering. Her heart could barely contain itself sitting next to that handsome man whose words were making her treasure chest sizzle for him even more. Glen's body was generating such an erotic craving between her legs, she needed to find a bit of relief. Kali flickers a sexy wink at Glen while ardently laughing. "I feel like we could sit here with me listening to your sweet poetic words all night. As my heart would never tire of it. But maybe we should save a bit of these thought-provoking words for tomorrow."

Glen mildly laughs while uttering. "I figure that's my cue to get out of the car and safely deliver you home."

Kali somewhat smiles, saying. "Unless you're staying the night, I suppose it is!"

Tonight was more than either Kali or Glen desired it to be. However, when the little rendezvous started, they each had incompatible notions going into this date. Yet, somewhere during these romantic sequences, the hearts caught a glimpse of something mystically unexpected. It was just what Kali desired, yet on the other hand, it was more than Glen could have ever bartered for; love!

Glen's spirit discovered this fiery passion in his heart which heatedly streams thru his veins for Kali. His core craves this fervid moment of romance tonight. As Glen sits anxiously beside Kali ravenously longing to tenderly stroke her silky body thru the wee hours of the night.

Even though; he desires Kali so, Glen recognizes his conscience wouldn't allow him to stay all night with her and still respect himself. He knows what he needs to do but Glen's having a difficult time saying good-night to a night of passion with Kali. Then he unhappily whispers. "Well, I suppose you're right; it might be time to go!"

As Glen clutch hold of the door handle, Kali catches onto his other hand somewhat pleading. "Please do not go, Glen, at least not yet!"

Kali's heart did not know how she would bear to see his car drive away tonight without her. Especially, when Kali still has so much more to share with him, including herself. Also, the desires of her femininity were starving for a blistering night of possibilities with Glen. How do Kali let Glen go when he sits beside her drooling with a sexiness that's arousing the petals of her flower below?

Glen's beguiling eyes were triggering this suffocating awakening at the junction of Kali's thighs while the soul requires a little bit more time with him. Because tonight she was ready to splash into these inviting waters of her store-bought lover. Kali tries to tempt Glen once again. "Are you positive you are ready to pass up on this night full of passion with me?"

Glen's manhood found it very difficult to believe his illogical master could deny it's pleasure. However, Glen didn't have any other answer than yes. Suddenly he was ready to give up on a night to quench his thirst with her for real love. Glen can only nod his head in response to Kali's question to avoid the escaping word from his lips from forming into a "no" instead of a "yes".

Even though Glen's response was yes; for now. Kali wasn't going to give up on him. Especially, when all the passions within her essence were bursting with so many requests. Even things she still desires to hear about him before he go. Kali's raging appetite needs to fulfill these dreams of her heart now. She can't see sleeping alone in her bed when Glen was eagerly sitting right across from her. Why should she snooze alone tonight when an able body man was there and willing? At least Kali thought.

Glen's entire soul is sensing the same passion as Kali is feeling. He slowly shifts in his seat trying to get a little bit nearer to Kali as he affectionately brushes her cheek lovingly uttering. "Kali, I don't want to, but I must go!"

Chapter Fourteen

*K*ali's core was sadden to hear Glen speak of leaving her. At that moment, it was something Kali didn't want to even consider as she breathes. "Just a minute more."

Glen gazes intensely within Kali's begging eyes as he tries to make her understand why he can't stay. "I never dreamed my life had room in it for you." Glen hesitates briefly while recognizing his heart has taken full control of his lips. "Yet, Kali, my heart desires you so much. In fact, at this moment I don't want our romantic night to end either; not without sampling your sweetness!"

Kali smiles as she lastly thought her and Glen are on the same page as she utters. "Glen, that is precisely how I feel!" She delicately inhales while glancing eagerly into his moving eyes. A pair of eyes which were so seductive that they stole her breath away while luring her inward.

Kali's heart knows Glen's essence isn't only thirsting a right now moment with her. Lastly, her soul realize he desires so much more; a lifetime of devoted moments.

Glen breathes tenderly, uttering. "I realize we've had some bumps in this path tonight. Yet, I desire a forever for us to be similar to those last hours of our life. What a romantic voyage I have experienced with overflowing passion filled with starry-eyed kisses between us."

"Oh, Glen!" Kali with bated breath utters. "What an amazing thing to hear. Although, I desire our forever to resemble so many ardent moment of our entire date."

Glen softly laughs asking, "I'm all ears, please do tell me, so, I can capture it over-and-over for you always."

"Glen, when you passionately embraced me in those strong, loving arms of yours on the dance floor and our lips tenderly met in such a romantic kiss." Kali's heart is overflowing with such a passion, as she heavily breathes outward to release the pinned up excitement before she goes on. "However, the moment when you passionately entwined our bodies closer while whispering tenderly in my ear that you had found your dream in me."

He glares at her affectionately uttering, "I remember that precise moment as if it was just now happening."

Kali breathlessly continues, "It was then that I knew it was the very words my ears desired. And, fervent kiss which my lips longed so for. A period in time, I want to live over-and-over again with you as my forever love!"

Glen eyes looks away from Kali. He knew this was a forever promise he could not possibly fulfill; not at that moment. Although; Glen's core was free to love Kali as she needed, but not his life since Jo-Ann still exists.

Leering into Glen's eyes; even now, her heart sensed that was the precise time when Glen's heart fell in love.

At least, for Kali, it was when love begun, and a core had changed. Kali realized the instant Glen's fervid eyes met with her eyes; it felt so right. However, as Glen rest his lips upon hers in such a passionate kiss. It was when she saw such love for her inside his eyes. Also, that way his essence abruptly needed to leave to avoid her touch. At that very instant, Kali knew Glen was trying so hard to refute those sensations of the heart for her. A scuffle Kali understands Glen's soul has presently lost since his spirit is already imprisoned from the fervor of the night for her.

Glen fires a sexy wink in her path, as he passionately affirms. "Kali, I believe at that exact moment was when I realized that I was falling in love with you. Right then, Kali, you transformed my heart for the very first time."

Kali softly whispers, "Glen, I know because I sensed your passion deep within my soul!"

"Yes, you made a new man of me," Glen leers at her with so much hunger inside for Kali. Regardless of how much Glen wanted to fight the sizzling emotions which set his whole world aflame, there was just no denying it. His heart and soul were indeed falling in love with Kali.

Kali breathes softly, uttering. "Glen, it definitely was not me. It was love which made a new man of you!"

Glen was a bit speechless by Kali's comeback. As he recognizes it must be love which suddenly reformed his way of thinking. However, whose love? Was it Kali's or the love of a higher power, God's?

Suddenly, Glen needs a bit of air, as he quickly grabs hold of the door handle. His brain starts to realize what his life has been like without God or Kali. Wordless, he turns to smile at Kali as Glen opens his door. He slowly steps both feet out of the car, at once. As his feet touch down together on the asphalt, Glen looks back in Kali's face recognizing no words were required. Besides, Glen senses she understood the depth of his appreciation for her heavenly love which he was feeling thru God! Right then, Glen's lips were smiling with an unforgettable joy, as he continues to get out of the car.

Glen slowly strides around to the passenger's side of the car, he woefully opens her door. He quickly spreads out his right hand to help Kali to her feet. Glen fervidly tightens the grasp on her hand while he walks with Kali side-by-side to her front door in silence.

Reaching Kali's doorway, Glen releases that grasp as he passionately turns her to face him. He stares into her radiant eyes in the moonlight. Glen's lips hungrily seeks out a pair of willing lips as he kisses Kali good-night.

Glen affectionately embraces Kali while he excitedly set her lips aflame with his sultry kisses. As their mouth unwillingly parts from their fiery touch, he avidly states. "It's getting harder and harder to leave you tonight!"

Kali softly whispers while tenderly brushing his face, "Then why not just stay!"

Glen's impulses below desire Kali so, but his heart is still saying no, as he let go of a weary sigh saying. "Kali, every inch of my being is fighting to stay." He fleetingly stops to take a breath of air, "Even though it is difficult to walk away from your passion, I must go! Particularly, while I still have the strength to do so."

Kali can sense Glen's thirsting for her eating away at his soul. It was such a penetrating emotion that was fast overtaking her essence as Glen softheartedly declares to Kali. "There are just too many rules for falling in love!"

Kali fervidly requests, "Why can't we just cast all our worries aside and fulfill our dream of joyful pleasures?"

Glen leers into Kali's face with such a burning desire for her as he utters. "You are making me a new man, so please don't tempt me to revert now; you might not like the other man." Glen heavily sighs, "Why not just leave our last spoken words; until tomorrow, as good-night!"

Kali leisurely kisses Glen on his cheek, as she frowns while emphasizing. "Good-night!"

Kali excitedly stares into Glen's gorgeous eyes as she removes the door key from her purse while her intellect probingly declares. "Don't think you got off easy after a tendentious remark like that one." Kali jokingly smiles!

Glen stares at Kali with that horrid goofy smile wide across his frowning face as that unrecognizable noise in his throat escapes his lips. "Mm-hmm!"

The tongue had misrepresented his thought process. Glen didn't mean to cast any alarms for Kali about that unpromising kind of man he was before meeting her.

Somewhat dismissing this notion of his remark, Kali quickly turns around to face her front door. Kali inserts her key into the keyhole unlocking the door. Though as Kali strides through her doorway, her core just couldn't imagine who the other man was that Glen was speaking of that she wouldn't like. Since the man who had stolen her heart tonight was so much more than she expected. Because the Glen, she had become to know and admire was so passionate, yet selfless with a loving heart.

In any case, she knew overthinking the matter would

just cause despair while undoing all that progress which they had accomplished tonight. Or perchance Kali only wishes to remember their date as it was, perfect!

Kali smiles as she rotates to face Glen. She delicately caresses his face within her hands while taking a second to contemplate on her and Glen's time together. As her mind quickly recognized before their romantic escapade tonight, it was only a taste of greed for Glen. Yet, it was merely the hot-blooded desire to soothe an itch for her.

A positive pathway for sin that evolved full circle for Kali and Glen as they first stopped to explore a stage of like for one another. A short-lived phase that grippingly captivated their passion for one another. A sensation so real, it made them victims of their own lustful games. A game of love, so intense, neither of them could fight its enraptured moments.

Although, she vowed to never fall in love with Glen; Kali couldn't stop it. As the air was so intoxicating with Glen's desire for her. She's having such a beatific night; one Kali only dreamed of having with Glen someday.

But what she didn't realize. It was a moment both of their lives were starving so greedily to behold. A chance to belong or just to be loved by someone. A small piece of joy that they both had sadly misplaced along the path to pursue happiness in other things. However, not Glen or Kali is prepared to realize what was missing has been found within each other; love.

Glen and Kali's heart knew what it desires. Although

Glen's eyes are blindsided from mind games of reprisal, Kali recognizes an incredible spark flaring among them.

A zealous sector within Glen's world which Kali had sort rights to be a part for so many years. Yet, tonight it was lastly tapping with a rhythm of love on Kali's door; after just one date.

Kali somewhat smiles asking. "Glen, I believe you're missing the sensations that I'm feeling. Can you feel the red-hot energies from the feverish connections between us, or is it just me on this enchanted expedition alone?"

Glen's eyes were filled with bliss as he states. "I have been going through life blindfolded until tonight." Glen pauses a second to contain his sense of passion for Kali before continuing, as his body was tingling all over with zeal. "If you're willing to take that chance on loving me, then I would be thrilled to take this journey with you!"

Kali smiles like a kid on Christmas morning who has just what they wanted all along, love. As Kali looks into a snapshot of what lies ahead for her and Glen, she says to him. "I feel such happiness within your lovable arms, so, this is one excursion worth exploring with you."

Glen slightly smiles as he draws Kali closer into such a sizzling embrace of their lips together.

The moments were filled with such a burning desire. Kali's heart didn't ever want to let go. She realizes Glen felt that excitement brewing in his essence among them as well from the tunefulness of his words. Nevertheless, Kali knows she is not trying to upset that precious twist of faith. Not when Glen's doubtful mind no longer was indecisive whether the heart preferred Kali's love rather than his own trust issue. A phase in his life, Kali's entire being has struggled so hard for Glen to overcome from the very day she set eyes on him. However, that intense moment was when she realized that Glen and her heart was lastly yoked together. Kali had finally achieved that long-awaited stage of love with him. Even if, she wasn't sure what the stars had in store for them, Kali's happier than she has ever dreamed possible with Glen.

Presently, Glen's full attention is in the same dreamy phase which Kali's was. Glen was ready to stake a claim to her same values and goals of life. Glen is prepared to make her priorities a part of his forever. One step in life which Glen never imagined taking with any woman.

Glen's quickly learning with Kali's affection and love by his side; but most important God's love, he was now finding his way in life again. Glen was joyfully regaining his misplaced soul which had vanished years ago due to his greediness for things which did not bring joy.

Right now, Glen's soul is rejoicing as he passionately states. "Good-night, Kali!" But since he wasn't ready to let go of Kali or the moment, he asks. "Could I call you when I arrive home to hear your voice one more time?"

She breathes tenderly asking, "Call me tonight?"

He intensely sighs, "Well, I suppose it is already late, so my heart must hold you close until tomorrow."

Resting her arms softly on Glen's neck, Kali gazes in his face passionately admitting. "Glen, if you only knew how much my heart hunger for you right now. Yet, I'm taking a chance on our tomorrows; so, we'll talk then!"

He enunciates with such conviction, "I understand it

might be hard to believe now, but there will be so many more tomorrows for us!"

Glen steps up into her doorway to get a bit closer, as he lovingly envelopes Kali's face between his hands. He zealously grins while seeking out her lips. Glen's mouth ardently connects with Kali's lips with such yearning.

Glen looked-for Kali to crave his warm cuddles long after their lips parted. He wants Kali to recognize it was just a good-night kiss but never good-bye. Glen needed Kali to remember how deeply his feelings were for her.

As their mouths are gradually separated, he leaps out of Kali's front entrance. Glen affectionately whispers to her. "Lots of tomorrows flowing with passionate, sweet kisses just like that one, I promise."

Before swirling about to close the door, Kali asserts, "I pray there are because I rather like the sight of you in my life and the kisses are not half bad either." She gives Glen a sexy wink while enthusiastically smiling

Chapter Fifteen

Glen excitedly smiles as he tenderly utters, "And you in mine, so until tomorrow Kali, good-night!" As words of promise softly echoes from his mouth, Kali's heart is soaring with happiness. She smiles in anticipation of so many tomorrow with Glen before she devotedly voices. "Until we speak again your love will contain my heart!"

Shutting her door delicately behind Glen, Kali whirls around leaning her backside against the door. She could still feel Glen's existence, not only in her heart but even harboring within the midair. As this subtle aroma of his cologne was filling her nostrils making Kali want him in his absence even more. Even if; in her heart-of-hearts, a stellar romantic moment tonight has passed, Kali awaits their tomorrow. Because Kali sees a glimmer of hope in Glen's soulful eyes which makes her believe in his every word. Now, she's looking forward to Glen's promise of never-ending days of starry-eyed kisses and fervid times together. Mostly, because Kali was sensing a restoration of joy returning to her life. She states delicately, "Thank you, Lord, for always being a vital part of my untrusting life. Even when I am unsure you continue to stay. Also, Lord, for an amazing date with Glen!" With a heart full of joy, she starts the happy dance upstairs for a night in dreamland with Glen.

Walking back to his car, Glen's soul was overflowing with a happiness that he didn't realize existed until now. After years of running away from any emotions that the heart offered. Glen's entire world had been mesmerized by the untainted love of a woman who loves him, too.

Glen was so happy, he did not want to even think of the possibility of anything going wrong; not this time in his life. Once in his life, Glen was confident during this time around a woman could love him, flaws and all.

Tonight, he doesn't care what type of neighborhood, which Kali lived in or her treasures, as he walks back to his car. Here and now, none of the old ways of thinking mattered to Glen any longer; only Kali's love. He didn't know what he had done to deserve such a heart of bliss or such an incredible adore. Yet, here in the splendor of Glen's essence, his soul yearns for Kali. A woman Glen barely knows, but after just one chance meeting of their hearts on the dance floor there's no turning back now.

Nearing the car, Glen climbs into the driver's seat as his face lights up the midnight sky with happiness. That life with a good woman he was meant to live was finally claiming his heart. Glen's lips erupt into a sincere smile on his face with bliss. A smile that speedily turns upside down into a frown of displeasure as Glen's brain brings to light his continuing saga with Jo-Ann. He realizes it's a matter that needs to be cleared up to hold onto Kali's love and respect.

However; tonight, he only wanted for a moment to savor in the glory of being in love and not worry about anything else.

Glen realizes tomorrow, he must face this music and tell Jo-Ann the complete truth of the matter. He merely would make known to her that he unintentionally fell in love while in the wrong place, but at the right time. Any case Glen must man-up and be honest with himself and Jo-Ann to earn his wings of respect for Kali.

Glen vocally tosses words about to say to Jo-Ann on his ride home. Glen's head was all over the place, yet he recognizes there's just no getting around him ringing up Jo-Ann. However, Glen thinks morning would possibly make better sense to telephone when everything will be more transparent to Jo-Ann. Glen doesn't feel he needs to call her at some unearthly hour of the night to let her know their season was over. Why add confusion on top of confusion when it will make more sense to Jo-Ann if he telephones her at a more reasonable hour. He knows that will definitely give him a bit more time to mull over this situation. As well as, a few hours longer to mentally prepare himself for whatever comes his way.

Arriving home, Glen appeared okay with the choices he had decided on. At least, until he grasped, it was part of an old stalling tactic of his when dealing with women and the truth. But if he indeed changed, then he needed to handle his state of affairs with Jo-Ann graciously and face-to-face, not over the phone.

Getting out of his car to enter the house all his brain could think about was his love for Kali. Glen desires so much to call Kali and share his entire life. Even the part about Jo-Ann with Kali. He must be the individual who breaks the news to Kali about Jo-Ann. Glen knows that sort of upsetting truths coming from anyone other than him would devastate Kali. Glen feels he's the individual that could make Kali understand what their love means to him. He desires to think about the repercussion from this issue a bit longer. Glen isn't entirely optimistic if he really made the best choice to ask Jo-Ann's forgiveness, and break-up before sharing his past with Kali. Even if, Glen thinks Jo-Ann had a right to hear the news first.

Although, here and now, Glen's mind wasn't sure of anything other than he love Kali. He tries to drift off to sleep, but this conversation with Jo-Ann tomorrow was weighing too heavily in his mind. Glen's brain forecasts pounds of staggering heartache overhead for him in the end. Therefore, Glen's praying after a good-night sleep, tomorrow would have a sunnier outlook for a chat with Jo-Ann as Glen whispers. "Yes, that's what we need!"

Both Glen and Kali went to sleep, so encouraged for their tomorrow. A day filled with passionate words, and fervent kisses. A day which would start the forever they both spoke of and desired so much with each other but only if Jo-Ann's heart recognizes he loves Kali; not her.

Glen's head is so besieged by sleep, he's overlooking Martha; who knows him and Jo-Ann's connection. One person who adores a bit of stirred up chatter before the coming of day. And, of course, there was a blinded Kali who hasn't got a clue about what was going on.

It was a perfect setting for trouble, which sometimes comes before the crack of dawn. Especially when Kali's friend is Martha Hayward, their social gossip columnist. And, Martha got up extra early to grab dibs on the local gossip lines before anyone else did; mainly Jameson and Glen. Because what Glen's mind fails to grasp, not only did Martha know, who Jameson Milo and Glen Monroe was, but she knew all their dirty little-kept secrets, too.

Nevertheless, Glen's heart is in love, and he is a man with a purpose and for once, not a tainted one. No one; not even, Springfield gossipers will prevent his securing a destiny with Kali. Glen was taking no chance on sleep as his tired eyes just wouldn't shut, so he decides to stay up all night. He figures that way he can get ahead of the gossip, who have nothing better to talk about than him.

At any rate, he needs to go discuss the situation with Jo-Ann and ask for her forgiveness. And, then continue on to Kali's house before anyone else did. Therefore, to speak, face-to-face with Jo-Ann, Glen telephoned her at the break of dawn pleading with her for a heart-to-heart over a cup of coffee. Thus, when Martha called Jo-Ann, Glen had just wrapped up his discussion and was on his way out the door. He was in a hurry to go see Kali right then and let her know that his heart and life is all hers.

Glen was bursting at the seams with happiness to be unrestricted to pledge his full heart and soul to the only woman he loves. Also, he's overwhelmed with knowing Jo-Ann's heart no longer requests for the desires of any man which does not want her. He's confident the joyful news will lively up Kali's morning with an air of ecstasy. Mostly, Glen understands his heart has been released to start living a new spirit within as a changed man to love Kali. A piece of news, he knew Kali wanted to hear.

Glen was finally free to share his entire life with Kali since Jo-Ann had set him free to love her. He is happier than he has been in a long time because Glen has found with Kali this taste of what a magical romance could be.

In his world, Glen never imagined a day like this one is conceivable for his broken heart. To be falling in love with Kali, his heart never dreamed it could be so happy.

Before dawn, Martha's lips starts her chatter. Martha hasn't spoken to Jo-Ann Parks in years, but today it was her civic duty to educate Jo-Ann about Glen. Mainly, in Martha's mind once a two-timer Glen will always be the philanderer. Therefore, he was not the least bit in Kali's or Martha's statuses as a perfect suitor for her friend.

Martha's fingers speedily enter Jo-Ann's digits in the phone all while a tiny voice reminds her it's wrong. Yet, another smaller voice keeps insisting to Martha, her call was the right thing to do. And, someday Martha felt her friend, Kali, will even want to thank her for superseding on her behalf to prevent a heartbreak.

Smiling, Martha waits on Jo-Ann to pick-up as every bit of consciousness she had starts to kick in. However, for Martha, it is a bit too late when she's already swayed her brain that she was doing the best thing for everyone involved. After all, she was protecting Kali from the life of shame with Glen as Martha questions herself. "Can't anyone else see a train wreck heading for Kali but me?"

Even though, Martha was always on this scavenge to

outdo everyone else with the latest gossip, she seems to target others. However, this once Martha is the topic of gossip herself as Jo-Ann finally answers Martha's phone call laughing. "Hey there girl, I thought this caller might be you ringing my phone off the hook."

Martha lightly chuckles while voicing. "Beloved, why would you be expecting me to call you?"

Jo-Ann laughs while stating. "Well, I was just talking with Glen. Yes, he told me how you played him and my boy, Jameson, last night." As the words of truth quickly flows, Martha nose turns up. Martha believes, she is too good to speak with Jo-Ann, yet Martha knows she must to help Kali. So, Martha asserts apprehensively. "Oh, so Glen already called you, and so early?"

Jo-Ann quickly comeback, "No, Glen is at my house having coffee with me right now. Would you like to talk with him?"

Martha's brain was going a mile a minute as she says, "Now why on earth would I want to speak with Glen?"

Jo-Ann clarified, 'Well, after all these years and given we were never chatting friends. So, I thought you might be out for a little gossip to see if Glen was here."

Martha's displeasure was raging as she replies. "Now you know I will not stay on the phone being insulted by the likes of you, Jo-Ann Parks!" As Martha slams down the phone's receiver, she was furious. You could almost see this puff of smoke coming out of her nostrils as she takes her hand off the phone thinking about Jo-Ann.

Jo-Ann exasperatingly groans out of annoyance with Martha while saying to Glen. "Martha never gave me an opportunity to clarify what's really going on among us."

Jo-Ann smiles in Glen's path knowing whatever saga she called to fabricate about him was already being told.

Glen avows, "Yes, and we both have first-hand scars to prove the power of that woman's tongue. It can start a massive war!"

Martha's chattering lips has all the ammo she needed on Glen. Martha's snooping is starting to prove a point that Glen has not changed. How could Glen be in Kali, and Jo-Ann's bed last night? Martha recognized Jo-Ann is trying to steer her off course by making up a lie about her and Glen just sipping on a cup of coffee.

Martha naughtily laughs because she realizes without a doubt that fresh bit of gossip; she acquired, will stop a rapid-firing train in its tracks. So confident with herself, Martha whispers softly. "Oh yes, with the new evidence available, it will indefinitely suspend any schemes which Mr. Monroe has up his sleeves." Martha excitedly sighs. "And, who could believe it just fell into my lap!" As she tries to quit gloating long enough to get a juicy story for Kali's ears to hear about Glen and Jo-Ann.

Martha's brain starts to add a few spicy details of her own to the Glen and Jo-Ann plainness. As she becomes sandwiched among the fine line of Martha's own reality of what Glen was doing. However, for Martha's head, it seemed more likely; than not, Glen stayed all night with Jo-Ann. If not factual, Martha didn't know why Jo-Ann was alluding Glen was having a bit more in his cup than coffee? Martha positions all her facts in her brain as she explores through her phone contacts for Kali's number. Martha's proud of herself as she prepares to call Kali to break the news about Glen

Monroe. However, she isn't aware Glen was not standing by to allow Martha to ruin his life again. Not this time, when Glen has changed his life to be part of Kali's.

The once for hire man, Glen Monroe, ceased to live. Glen is coming off the seasonal market. Glen's ready to hang a "Do Not Approach Sign" about his neck for the new lady in his life; Kali Mathias. As his mind considers a new leaf on life, Glen happily continues his crusade to woo Kali's heart. Glen flatteringly laughs at himself. He playfully states. "Ladies, all seasonal passes are now null and void. They're being revoked in the name of love."

Smiling, Glen could barely contain himself in his car seat. Riding along, Glen's spirit was in ecstasy and ready for all the life-altering changes necessary. Glen so wants to turn over a new leaf on life for a journey of love with Kali. At least, until Glen rides up in front of her door.

Chapter Sixteen

Glen wouldn't believe what his eyes were beholding. How could Glen believe his eyes? Glen shakes his head in disbelief as he asks. "Lord, please tell me it isn't so?"

Glen has just arrived in time to cast his eyes on such a nightmare while he was mindful. How could anyone's eyes ever recover from this horrible betrayal when so in love. Glen's heart might not ever mend from seeing the woman of his future, again, in the arms of another man. As he sits watching Kali; the lady Glen desires, standing beautiful as ever, yet passionately enveloped in the arms of a man; other than him.

Glen's heart along with his forever dreams melted in the vision of his soul. Even though he had no idea who the other man was it's such a blow to his ego as he asks himself. "Did she ever mention a boyfriend or husband during our date last night?" Glen's heart was crumbling. Temporarily, his essence was just too overcome to even comprehend if Kali had mentioned it. And, now Glen's incapable of thinking plainly as he harbors the offended soul from an eyeful of seeing Kali in this compromising situation. Specially, when it was an area of his life where Kali rested less than eight hours ago in his arms.

Glen's head was swarming with envy as he implores. "How would Kali even tolerate another man so close to her body; less alone, touching all over her body as if she belongs to him?"

His brain just could not wrap around the idea of this other man embracing Kali when she alleged to love him so last night. At first, Glen thinks it's all in his head. He was only imagining it all, yet that sight was etched in his brain. It wouldn't go away, and nothing he did seems to be working, as he sits immobilized in his car just staring at Kali. Glen rationally tries to eliminate such images of Kali which were haunting him now. Nevertheless, those sector of Glen's essence which loves Kali, it continually shows that portrayal of her in the arms of someone else other than him. Not only, was his sight capturing a clad male holding Kali so close they barely had room for air to breathe; she's wearing a negligée and bathrobe.

Glen tries hard to reason within as he thinks about a few factors. Although the sinful side of him keep trying to find a dark twist on what Glen was observing. As his eyes become fixated in a visionless stare, Glen begins to mull over the thoughts racing in his mind. *Perhaps if Kali were dressed, it would not have looked so suspect. No matter how hard I try to wrap my brain around this lustful action; it appears Kali had just gotten out of her bed. A love shack from where Kali is hugging and seeing her lover off at the front door. There's merely no other way to see that matter. But why would Kali pretend to be in love with me last night, perhaps a night of passion? How could I have been so foolish to fall for her games in the first place when I had already caught her in one suspicious act last night?*

Glen's heart was breaking to know another woman's deceit had made such a fool of him again? His head was soaring all over the place as his essence is bleeding for a little of God's mercy, as he whispers softly. "Lord, did I deserve such cruelty from Kali? Why are you letting this happen to me again when you know my heart so well?"

At that moment, he couldn't understand how such a loving God, would permit that same story to be written twice for his life. Because, Kali might not have known a broken heart, but God knew and still let it happen.

The way Glen's soul is grieving, he could not believe he was willing to alter his life for Kali. The first woman, who he has finally opened his heart to completely, since his misery. Kali was someone he trusted enough to lend his entire heart with a promise of a forever. He lifelessly rocks his head while muttering to himself noisily. "And, to think, I laid all my heart out there with the belief Kali could truly love me faithfully as I would her."

Glen realized his life wasn't flawless. Yet, he thought Kali was this one who would truthfully still love him, in spite of all his faults. However; from the look of things, Glen's detecting their situation is like the pot calling the kettle black. Since both, he and Kali had hidden secrets.

He could not wrap his mind around whose surprises were worst. Was it him not sharing with Kali the details about Jo-Ann or maybe her not sharing the undisclosed lover on the side. A lie well kept under cover from him.

Glen tussles profoundly within his heart for a reason which might satisfy his answer for why Kali couldn't be as he imagined her. A beautiful, yet an affectionate lady who would be trustful to the end. A woman, who could be entrusted with his core not to return it shattered into tiny little pieces. Right now, Glen's image of seeing Kali in someone else's arms has devastated his perception of what real love looks like as he asks God. "If Kali wasn't a woman to restore my heartbreak from You. God, lead me to one that could?" Glen dismally sits waiting God's reply, because he needed so desperately to understand a reason for this heartbreak. Because; if not, it would take Kali a lifetime to make him understand what he has just seen. And, much more for Kali to regain his trust. Even though, in his gut, he already realizes she could not; in a million years, explain her way out of this mess or did he care to hear the lies. Glen laughs as he asserts. "Besides, what could she say when my sad eyes already previewed a sample of Kali's secret life!"

With an extra heavy heart, he still sits there mooning over what would have happened. Yet instead, this spirit was beholding a case of stolen love as the man removes his arms from around Kali, suddenly walking away.

For a split second; the way Kali looks around before shutting her door, he hoped her eyes were desiring him.

However, as Glen starts to duck down in his vehicle, he recognizes that was merely her everyday style of closing the door. Because when Kali pushed her door shut, not once, did she even sense Glen's presence sitting outside her house. Unexpectedly, in his soul, Glen understands, he was oblivious to Kali; not a part of her today.

Glen's heart is racing so fast as he observes this man getting into his car driving away. When abruptly, Glen's legs wanted to rush up to Kali's front door and find out why he wasn't enough for her. Or perhaps why was she in the arms of another man when he loves her so. Right then, Glen's so confused that he doesn't realize what to say to Kali or whether it was best to just say nothing.

As the thoughts appeared to grow more and more in his mind, Glen becomes fixated. It was as if he woke up to someone else's life, today. Perchance, he really needs to go back home, and just restart this day all over again. Since the tomorrow, he spoke of for today, indisputably wasn't the promise he desired for another day. His core visualized days more filled with mystical dreams of their life of forever together. And, the inception here doesn't have visions for their future or any expectancy for Kali, or him. Glen tenderly murmurs, "Lord, not at all what I was expecting when I promised Kali a tomorrow?"

Glen wasn't sure how to make this day right for Kali and him. But what Glen was sure of is the woman, who professes to be in love with him, his eyes caught layered deep inside the fervent arms of another.

Glen's fully aware it's only been one night of passion filled by one fantastic date. But, what he feels for Kali is just as real as the shared joy on a Christmas morning.

For Glen, it was that kind of sensation inside of him which made a crooked man desire to give up his wicked ways. And, even if the romance stars did not align in his favor this time, a woman's love has changed Glen. Kali, who he met last night has made him want to be a better man. Love has finally conquered his colorful green life.

Still sitting brooding over his feelings for her, Glen's cell phone begins to loudly buzz. He sluggishly stares at the phone as he whispers. "If my heart has not suffered enough, it's Kali calling to crush my dreams forever!"

Glen sits there motionlessly as the racket from Kali's phone clattering appears to sever his core in two. It was as if the vision of her name as it displayed on his screen was reaching deep within his soul cutting off his breath. Its sudden loud clatter was immobilizing both his hands as Glen's entire body appears to be frozen. The essence of his spirit just wouldn't allow Glen to pick-up her call. Glen groans as his buzzing cell phone continue to echo the sound of her name within his ears over-and-over.

Glen's soul ached too much to speak to Kali. He did not have the heart or stomach to even hear meaningless words from her tongue. Glen's ears could not bear such empty excuses when all of his essence is desiring Kali at that very moment. For, Kali was the only woman which has ever spellbound him. She had captivated Glen's full body and soul as if his heart was in a honeymoon phase with Kali. It was such a fervent, yet intense kind of love which was so unforgettable to him. For once, Glen was not taken by a woman's money, since Kali's passion has awaken a new sensation within his heart. One that Glen wasn't ready for this story to end, even if it does exist in his mind only. Nonetheless, Glen believes if he answers Kali's call, it will douse that blazing flame forever.

Possibly someday, even later today, Glen knows that he must admit to Kali what his eyes detected. However, with the anguish inside his essence, it shouldn't be now. Since the poetry which might escape his tongue, at such a time, weren't the lyrics he cared to sing to his beloved without much thought. Especially, since Glen still loved Kali more than his core or words are willing to express.

Glen realizes he needs an escape. Glen's heart wants time away to think. Because, right then, the one woman he truly cared so much for; Glen suddenly had no vocal sound left for her. How was Glen going to tell her what his core was feeling when he was so uncertain? Since all these promises Glen vowed to Kali for their tomorrows were now filled with shattered unbeliefs. At present, his heart has been assured the sort of starry-eyed futures of a forever doesn't exist; at least, not for him and Kali.

However, still watching Kali's name gleaming across his screen, Glen recognizes he's truthfully falling in love with Kali. Thus, his essence cannot put aside the tender suffering of his soul long enough to still want Kali back in his life. Glen gently mumbles, "How is it possible for my heart to ever trust Kali or any woman again?"

Suddenly, Glen's heart recognize if he couldn't trust Kali, he would never love again. Finally, he noticed the old Glen has matured overnight, but he wasn't sure this is what he bargained for. Not, if Glen couldn't have her to share part of his life. At first, Glen would not portray his life with Kali, now he can't imagine it without her.

Glen glances at Kali's name flashing cross his phone screen as it persists to ring and ring. Finally, he switches on the ignition. While Glen pulls off from the curbside, Kali receives a beep on her phone. Anxiously, she clicks over hoping it was Glen calling her back. Kali adds a bit of sex appeal to her talk. "Why, hello there handsome! I have been trying to reach you. Where are you?"

Martha teasingly states. "From the sound of things, I am going to take a wild guess and assume Glen was not your overnight boarder."

"Oh, hello Martha," Kali agitatedly voices. "Did you need something because I'm a little busy right now?"

Martha tries so hard not to expose Glen too soon, as she breathes heavily asking. "He's not there with you?"

Kali replies sharply. "No, did you need something?"

Martha smiles! As the "No" sung from Kali's tongue was the precise answer, she wants to hear. Martha sucks in air through her teeth, then devilishly grinning, asking. "Oh, beloved, is Mr. Glen missing in action already?"

Kali retorts, "Martha, I really don't have time for the dog and pony show you displayed last night, so why are you calling?"

Martha giggles friskily. "Quite the opposite, I am the bearer of news this morning. Maybe, it's something you just might want to know about your Glen Monroe."

Kali disturbingly sighs, but still quite curious to what Martha's lips has to say. "What news could you possibly have which will interest me about Glen?" Kali grumpily laughs, "When last night, Martha, you pretended not to recognize who he was. Well, at least, you acted out that part quite tastefully!"

After Kali's small sermon, Martha becomes nervous, as she nosily begins an interrogation of Kali. "Beloveth, what lies could Glen's wayward tongue have said to you for your lips to recite such a thing?"

Kali, noticing Martha on edge decided to clown with

her a little. "Glen was speaking his truth about the three of you which surprisingly included Jameson Milo, too."

Martha was frightened that Glen had said something to Kali about her and Jameson. Because Martha realizes from Kali's gleaming charm as she answered her phone, there was no way Glen had bared the Jo-Ann history to Kali. As Martha impatiently appeals. "Why, what did he have to say about Jameson and me because it's all lies?"

Kali, now more interested than ever, she asks. "Why is there something Glen should have told me about you and him?"

Martha becomes a little more calm because, after the question opposed by Kali, she realized Glen hadn't told Kali anything about her and Jameson. As Martha laughs softly, "Glen and Me! Sweetie, you're delusional to even consider such a thing!"

Kali's brain snaps into overdrive as she recollects the dialog where Glen admitted to knowing Martha. So, she realizes if Martha knows, she'll reveal all of Glen's past.

Chapter Seventeen

Kali, trying to learn more about Glen's past life from Martha, she queries. "Well, Glen did say the two of you knew one another many years ago."

Martha naughtily laughs, "Hum, so Mr. Glen did tell you he knew me. Well, what else did his lying lips say?"

Kali was getting a bit perturbed, after all, Martha was speaking about her new found love. She boldly requests of Martha. "Just what are you trying to say, Martha?"

Martha was just waiting for that invitation from Kali to tell it all. "I'm just saying, Glen might not be the man who your heart believe him to be after just one date."

Kali is suddenly listening with both ears, as she asks. "What do you mean? Why derail my feelings now when Glen desires me; I even believe it might be love?"

Martha's mind was blown away that Kali actually did believe Glen loved her. At this moment, Martha needed her friend Kali, and not that one who loves Glen. Since, right now, she wanted to trust Kali with the whole truth about how her, Jameson, and Glen actually first met.

At the same time, Martha realized her past escapades were scandalous. How would that shame permit Martha to even speak of her past life with Kali; especially, if she stands a chance of losing it all? Martha senses she'll lose Kali, the only real friend she has left, to Glen again.

Nonetheless, Martha's getting even with Glen meant more than losing Kali's trust of her. Martha couldn't let Glen oust her out of Kali's life. Not as he once did with her best friend, Jameson. Martha felt Glen had taken so much from her when he convinced Jameson not to take her back after the affair. And, Martha's angry side needs to make Kali pay for Glen's mistakes as she asks. "How can you love Glen, so intensely, after just one date?"

Kali stares into open space, as she declare to Martha. "I realize it's all happening so fast, but Martha, the man who wined and dined me with such passion last night. I am truly falling in love with him. And, remember I have truly loved Glen a lifetime already; so it wasn't hard."

Martha breaks a moment, then she asserts. "Perhaps it's just not suppose to be between you and Glen."

"Martha!" Kali impatiently questions. "What are you even saying? Because; trust me, it's much too late for us to back away from each other now; not after our date."

Kali was thinking, *how would she possibly walk away from a thriving love like hers and Glen's, no matter what he did?*

Abruptly, without giving it a second thought, Martha can't help herself as she averts Kali's thinking. "Do you know where your beloved Glen was last night?"

Kali didn't understand what Martha's asking her; not when less than eight hours ago Martha crashed her date with Glen. A bit confused, Kali asks. "Martha, your not making any sense, what exactly are you asking me?"

Martha lightly breathes in some air, then exhales out. "Well, when I'm done you will undoubtedly understand and recognize just how his spots has not changed. Glen is still the same ruthless man which I once knew."

Kali's uncertain whether she even wants to know the lies resting on Martha's tongue, but her heart does. Kali remorsefully asks. "What spots and what sort of person was the Glen you knew before?"

Martha rapidly says. "He's just a woman's boy toy of the season; a Casanova. That's the Glen, I knew!"

Kali's heart begins to race, as she couldn't imagine if the lies were true which appears to echo throughout her eardrum. Kali just wants to turn-off the horrible sounds ricocheting off Martha's lips into Kali's heart. However, Kali could not keep from wondering where's the proof. Since Martha had been faking to be one of Springfield's ladies who lust for Glen over the years. When suddenly, Martha knows Mr. Glen Monroe's life story to cast.

Kali questions Martha's lies to uncover if there was a speck of truth to her allegations. Frustrated, Kali shouts into Martha's ear. "Where's your proof? And, how long have you been concocting your little juicy gossip for me to close my heart to Glen?"

"Kali, I hate that I'm the friend breaking the news to you about your new lover. Besides, Glen already has the one girlfriend, so how can he ever truly belong to you."

Quite taken back by Martha's newsflash, Kali asserts boldly. "And, how would you possibly know that?"

Martha goes on, "Well, there is so much more to the story since Glen stayed all night with her after your date last night. Perhaps, he forgot to mention that to you."

Kali will never understand why Martha was trying to hurt her so when she pretends to be a friend. Wiping an infuriating tear which starts to form at the left corner of her eye, Kali asks. "What's your proof, and how do you know Glen has a girlfriend or stayed there last night?"

Martha breaks out with this little white lie which was only partly right since she leaves out the parts about her and Jameson. "Well, when I last spoke to an old friend, named Jo-Ann Parks, she was dating Glen." She stalls a few seconds trying to be extra careful not to mix any of her words as Martha continues on breaking Kali's heart. "Well, I buzzed to check on Jo-Ann before sun-up, and to my shock, she was too busy to talk. And, that's when Jo-Ann shouted out that she and Glen was sipping their morning cup of coffee together."

Kali did not want to trust Martha's lies; not with that fabricating track record she has. Kali asks. "So, I should just believe you? Please, a social chat to get some gossip on Glen because that's what you do, always meddling!"

Martha shyly giggles. "So, you got me on that one. It was quite noticeable as I accidentally drove by your way this morning, and noticed Glen's car wasn't there."

"Martha!" Kali barks into the phone. "Of the things, which you have done to me, I believe this is the worst."

Martha's tone mellows as she really tries to persuade Kali it was all done out of love for her. "I knew that old Glen was a snake in the grass, so, I was making sure the weasel was not going to hurt you; my dearest friend."

Kali tries to calm down a bit before she tells Martha, "A man you pretended not to know for years, during all the time we have known one another, yet now his book of life stories come to light." Kali pauses, as she exhales asking. "Where was all the advice when I told you upon my move to Springfield how I desired Glen Monroe?"

Martha hurriedly voices. 'Oh, beloved at such a time, Glen was way out of your league. So why would we fret over the impossible? I felt no need, until now to let you know his real sides to life!"

Kali couldn't believe her ears, but why should she be astonished by anything which rolls off Martha's lips. It's no secret what Martha always thought of Kali, although the naked truth still hurts. Kali's obviously left wordless from Martha's ignorant words. Kali hurriedly ends their call saying. "Martha, I always knew you were not a truth bearing friend, but I tolerated you. But that little exploit might have severed our friendship to a state of unrepair for now; maybe forever!"

Martha starts to beg and plea to avoid losing her one and only friend now that she doesn't have Jameson. Yet this time, it might have been too late as Kali rapidly lays down the receiver to a tone of silence in Martha's ear.

Hearing the inaudibility on the other end of her line, Martha restlessly sighs while whispering. "I know Kali's pride is wounded. However, Kali will be thanking me in a few weeks for the news on Glen's ugly untruthful side of life. Perhaps, Kali just needs a little while to sulk, and then I will ring her up for a chat." She dejectedly smiles!

Kali realizes that closeness she and Martha once had was irreparable. Yet, on the other hand, not the rapport she and Glen shared. Kali's heart wouldn't believe Glen was the sort of man who could treat her so horrible and cruel. It was impossible for the Glen, she was so in love with. Nevertheless, if it was true, those were words only believable coming from Glen's lips; real or not.

Within Kali's soul, she knows not to believe anyone, who was jealous and conniving as Martha; mainly, if the lies were about Glen. Since Kali realizes he was the sort of soulmate and friend, who could be committed to her until she respired her last lungful of air. Those were just the feelings of her heart about him; even after one date. Kali knowingly rumors, "Somethings a girl just knows!"

Abruptly, she finds herself questioning her own core while noisily huffing. "How could Glen not be the right one for me?" She somewhat frowns with uncertainty.

Even though, after Joseph, Kali never gave her heart the proper amount of time to heal before Glen. She felt it wasn't a mistake that her essence turned to Glen. The one man, who she knew would fulfill all her unexpected missing flaming desires taking away by Joseph.

Kali figured God recognized the torture of her heart long before she did. However; once again, she's praying God was the One, which turned her heart toward Glen. And, not her own selfish desires, as Kali tenderly utters. "God, it had to be You to send Glen. I believe, no One besides You, Lord, knew my hurt from losing Joseph!"

Kali had much faith to know only God felt her pain.

Therefore, Kali actually needs to believe God sent Glen to her. If no other purpose than the fact, her trust was a bit wavered in the love department with the Lord. Even though Kali still prays with every breath within for God to give her a chance at real love. A plead of passion that appeared so similar to the one she first had experienced with Joseph Carlson. Even if, during the cheating hours of Kali and Joseph's rapport, she recognized he was not her man sent from God. Then again, how could Joseph fulfill her heart's desire when her body and soul still lust for Glen. Kali can't believe she had deprived herself for six months of Glen's love while going thru the motions of caring for Joseph. She breathes. "Why had I misused precious months in time with the wrong man?" Even if, Glen was the man, who was always beyond the reach of her financial boundaries for ages; her Mr. Unsustainable Man. And, for so long, the only way Kali's fervent heart imagined befriending Glen's money-made side was thru her starry-eyed thoughts. Nonetheless, here was Glen, a man Kali's heart couldn't ever envision wanted her. But without a word, she succeeded at spell-bounding Glen's untamed soul making him avidly desire the lady in red.

Kali's forsaken essence just recognized Glen was the only man who even spoke about a tomorrow. Or giving Kali the kind of dedicated relationship she prayed for in a man's life. Glen's the first man to faithfully avow such devoted love to Kali! Something no man had ever done before him nor did she want to do after him because he was the only one her heart desired forever.

Thus, Kali was not going to permit herself to believe this worst-case scenario about Glen. Even though it did seem a little dismal right then, Kali's going to trust him.

Kali's core needed so much to give him a fair chance before flying to her own assumption. So Kali continued to telephone Glen every hour on the hour with the high hopes of them having a tomorrow. Because all he needs to do was tell her Martha's words were full of lies. Thus Glen's cell just keep ringing and ringing in her eardrum. In her mind, she wouldn't believe a man which claimed to love her profoundly was currently missing in action.

Why was Glen missing when Kali needed him most? How would Kali ever prove to Martha that she's wrong about Glen when Kali had no clue where he was. Kali's head was exhausted with probing, yet without searching for Glen, there wasn't any other means for her to verify his innocence.

Quite worried, Kali swiftly combs through her purse that she carried last night for clues where Glen could be as she gasp for some air. She didn't know what to think as Kali frowns, asking herself. "What could I have done to make Glen retract his feelings from me?" Kali loudly moans. "It just can't be happening, not now when Glen and I were so close to having it all; true love!"

Kali's mind was swimming with all sorts of thoughts as she wards-off those senseless words of Martha's lips. While breathing gradually, Kali tries to stop the baseless accusations which appear to race about inside her brain, as Kali gently asks, "Glen where are you? Because these words continue to control my thoughts until your voice can set my mind free with the truth!"

Though; Kali's heart is shattered to hear such things, she knows there is many sides to every story. But, those falsities which Martha spoke were about Glen. The man

Kali is suddenly realizing she has no future without him in her life; how can she dream of loving someone else.

Kali's fulfilled life solely is invested in Martha's truth being a bunch of lies. Yet, without Glen how would she ever get to know his side versus Martha's? Truth or not, Kali recognizes other than God there is just one person who knew the real facts. And, that person unexpectedly vanished without a single word.

Kali starts to pray for an answer, as she humbly asks. "God, if Glen was in fact sent by You, then why can't I find him?" Just as Kali concludes her prayer, she has an inkling where Glen could be. So, without hesitation, she promptly strolls over to the front door pushing her feet inside her pair of shoes sitting near the door. She opens the door, as her right-hand picks up the car keys from a nearby stand while briskly heading out to her car.

Chapter Eighteen

Kali had no idea where her little venture could guide her since she had no inkling where Glen lived. But what she did know about Glen's life might lead her to him.

Kali realizes wherever the trail took her, she's willing to travel it until Glen was safely back. She's praying that knowing where Glen worked would deliver him right in her waiting arms.

Kali knows his place of work was her only chance at verifying all of Martha's mendacities were just that, lies.

Because there's no way, Kali could permit Martha to come between this new found love. Kali cared for Glen too much. Kali's moment with Glen; last night, was her best time ever shared with a man outside the bedroom.

Loving Glen brought a pleasure within Kali's soul. It felt similar to the ecstasy that enthralls one's heart when waiting for your loved one at the airport terminal after a long journey. For Kali, it was a rush to her heart like no other feelings she has ever felt for a man.

And, the passion is still electrifying within Kali's ears from Glen's last spoken words to her. Just the sound of it was sending shivers all up and down Kali's spine with tingles of passion. How could Kali possibly let Glen get away from her now or ever; not without a good fight?

She was bewildered, yet unhappy at the same time to see how Glen was throwing their love all away. Because why would a man, who not only avowed to fulfill Kali's life with tomorrows full of their aspirations and dreams just go missing. This just does not make sense to her. If Glen's desires no longer wanted a lifetime of hopes and dreams for a forever with Kali; as much as she did, why didn't he just say so? She lightly sighs of bewilderment!

Kali sadly asks herself. "How could Glen's heart just fade away from our love? Particularly when Glen's core was only apart from mine just a few hours."

Kali was utterly baffled as she softly moans, assuring herself. "There must be some rational explanation for it all because I know Glen's heart and soul was all mine as the date ended." Suddenly, her mind begins to think all kind of catastrophic things which might have happen to him. Kali's brain was overflowing with concerns, as she respires forcefully averring to herself. "Glen might have been in some sort of accident because he is just not that cold-hearted to make me worry over him so intensely!"

Whatever Glen's motives were Kali's going to figure it out. Opening the car door, Kali hops inside. Buckling up, she takes off from the curbside while softly inhaling and bearing in mind. *What if Glen doesn't desire to be found? What if all the things Martha was saying about him were real?*

Kali hurriedly clears her head of the "what if" verses which was taking over her thoughts. If she was going to confront Glen with Martha's falsehoods, her head must be functioning sensibly.

Right then, Kali really needed to transfer all Martha's foolish negative energy into positive notions. Because it was driving her crazy not knowing the truth. Kali didn't recognize if she was coming or going as her car speedily appears to robotically pivot off the road. Without being watchful of her own actions, her car just switches into a parking area at the Hay-Way Market where Glen works.

As the car come to a complete stop, Kali glances out over her steering wheel seeing where she was. Her heart quickly senses a bit of fear as Kali asks herself. "What if I walk into a place where all my hopes and dreams were going to be shattered?"

She knows her core can't take the disappointment of not being wanted to be found by Glen. So, Kali just sits in the parking lot gazing at the front door of the market praying for Glen to walk out at any second.

With a heart bursting with hope, Kali's eyes swell up with tears. Kali could not imagine when her feelings for Glen became so intensified. Nonetheless, were the tears which streamed down Kali's face really for him or more because she couldn't prove Martha was a two-faced liar.

Kali wasn't sure how the storyline with her and Glen is going to end; whether together or apart. But this very moment, the only thing she desires was to be within his passionate arms embraced in a fervent kiss. Because for Kali, she was not praying for a Romeo and Juliet ending for their love story. Not when Kali so desired Glen and her essence of burning passion to live infinitely without ever ceasing while their two hearts beat as one.

All of her bottled up emotions seem to be strangling Kali alive. Her thoughts were so jumbled that Kali feels forsaken. Kali needed just a few words of wisdom from her older sister, Lynette to assure her Glen will return.

Kali's eyes leer upward after reaching for her cell off the car seat. She sees Martha smiling while prancing out of a side door to Glen's workplace. Martha's face glows while wearing a somewhat dubious grin painted all over it sinfully. As Martha strolls back to her car tipping and peeping about much like a cat who ate her canary.

Kali was astonished, as she sits there with her mouth jarred open. Kali sneakily peeps over her steering wheel at Martha getting into her car driving off. Kali's irritated she ever thought of a snake-like Martha as a friend at all when the cards of mistrust were piled before her eyes.

Kali's brain was soaring as she hurriedly punches her sister Lynette's digits into the cell phone. Kali's irritated as Lynette answers the phone uttering "Hello! I see you finally got around to calling your big sister after such an exciting night out with Glen!"

Tearfully Kali replies. "Hey, Sis!" Tenderly rubbing a small tear which is forming at the corner of her left eye, she hesitates before going on. "How are you today?"

Lynette sensing a sadness in Kali's voice, she asserts. "What's wrong since it's obvious you did not call just to see how I was doing today?"

Kali unhappily asks. "Am I so transparent even over the phone to you?"

Lynette gently laughs. 'Sis, out with it. What did your Mr. Glen do?"

Kali quickly starts to speak. "Well, I don't suppose it is Glen, who has done anything. It's the untruthful tales which Martha called with this morning."

"Kali!" Lynette softly voices. "Why are you believing a single word which comes out from Martha's mouth?"

Kali slowly comes back. "Lynette, these lies Martha's spreading today is about Glen after showing her face up at our date last night pretending not to know him!"

Lynette breathes gently saying. "Kali, I don't need to listen any further, yet I do want to know. "Who are you trying to form this relationship with Martha or Glen?"

Kali slightly laughs, replying. "Of course Glen!"

Lynette underlines. "If it's Glen, Kali how could you listen to anything Martha has to say!"

Kali declares shamefully. "I suppose you are right; as usual, again you have set me straight on the bizarre, and selfish life of Martha."

Lynette sprouts outward. "Kali, just start listening to the sound of your own soul and not Martha. You could be pleasingly surprised by what it tell you about Glen."

All the things Lynette was saying, she already knows, yet it was just hearing it from Lynette that made it right, as she whispers. "Thank you, I will do just that!"

Lynette laughs while saying. "Now get off the phone and go get your truths from Glen." Even though; she is still sensing Kali was not revealing it all, Lynette did not want to meddle as she continues. "And, when we speak again, I want to hear a smileful tone in your voice."

As Kali and Lynette said goodbye and sharply ended their call, Kali was finally confident enough to go inside the store. She switches off her car to go face the drama. Even so, she lingers there for a while in awe pondering. *How could that changed man, who I came to understand and love last night already be two-timing me? Lord, say it isn't true!*

Kali never guessed she was asking too much of Glen in a relationship. All Kali required was that kind of love from Glen which contained all the passionate thrills she had with Joseph. But, minus Joseph's wandering eye for her friends or neighbor. These were Kali's requirements at first when she sought-after Glen since Joseph had set her aside for another woman. Then, her core hoped-for no more from Glen; however, at such an upsetting time in her life, no less from him either. Thus after one date, Kali felt as if her heart was getting much more than she could have ever imagined of Glen's love in one night.

Because for once, in this life, Kali's heart was feeling something a lot more tangible with Glen which was not money driven or lustful. But a love Kali could reach out and touch in the wee hours of the night and know Glen will be right there. It was an unremarkable sensation for her to realize God had finally answered her every prayer for just a chance at love. And, God has blessed her with one night with a passionate man, Glen. This man which truly desired to know the real Kali Mathias, and become to love her; the woman with flaws and all.

Kali couldn't believe, it begun with a captivated look into each other's eyes while dancing. A happening filled with a spellbinding passion over Kali and Glen, as both of them, dance cheek-to-cheek while nestled up in each other's fervent arms to her favorite song "At Last"!

When the music first started to play, Kali's heart was spellbound by such a caring man who could express his devotion so publicly. However, when Kali discovered it was Glen, she recognized that store-bought man, which she knew no longer existed. Somehow, the favor of that romantic meeting of Kali and Glen's heart on the dance floor sealed his passion for her. A sensation Kali's mind was going to hold onto until Glen was safely given back into the arms which were missing him most.

Even if Kali wanted Glen back so severely she could almost taste it, the warm and fuzzy feelings she's having was somewhat fading. It was a small struggle, at present to hold on to a man's warmness when it seem he wasn't trying to be found. Kali inhales softly as she wipes away all her new blissful sensations. Meanwhile, that status of Glen missing in action was tearing at the heart, trying to prove Kali's confidence in him to be wrongly placed.

Kali heard Glen's tales as an unworthy man who the highest bidders got the opportunity to stroll on his arm. But, within her essence, Kali realizes that was no longer the Glen she loved so. Therefore, how could Glen look Kali deep within her eyes and lie while at the same time confessing his love for her without even saying a word?

Kali believes beyond that closed door hides all those answers her core dreamed to hear right now. Therefore, after an hour of much deliberation, Kali's essence starts to speak to her mind while rubbing away all of Martha's lies one-by-one. Kali didn't realize if this action was due to her love for Glen or that sight of Martha coming out of his place of work. Nevertheless, whatever it was, it lit a burning fire within Kali's soul to go get her man.

Kali swiftly removes her hand off the steering wheel, opening up her car door. Kali steps out quickly without any delay. Kali promptly begins her walk forward so the mind would not conjure up any notion of uncertainty in her plan to see if Glen was at least working.

Slowly strolling through the front doors of Hay-Way Market, Kali sensed a numbness. A feeling of aloneness which seems to haunt her soul with every step she took.

Suddenly, Kali becomes motionless since in her view there was no Glen to be found nowhere. Standing there in the middle of an aisle looking rather daft while trying to fight back her tears. Kali begins to question her heart as she tries to avoid sobbing over this matter which she had no control over. "How would Glen just wander off and leave me this way?" Kali does not have this answer to her question. But she was going to find out if it takes every last breath she has. As these words softly rolls off her lips, Kali glimpses up into the face of a man coming toward her. Her frowning face swiftly goes to a smile as she asks. "Excuse me, sir, but do you know where I can find Mr. Glen Monroe?"

The man leers at her a minute before expelling. "Oh, Mr. Monroe left on an unexpected holiday! And, he will contact you on his return, but Mr. Monroe did leave me in charge. I would be delighted to assist you?"

Kali was in a state of puzzlement. Because what Kali thought her ears were hearing from this man just didn't seem right. What Kali heard oozing from the man's lips must be wrong. It had to be wrong as she stands before the man insisting on knowing where Glen Monroe was.

Kali pleads with this man. "Please, could you tell me where Glen Monroe is or at least give me his address?"

The man looks at Kali feeling a bit sorry for her, but at that same time, it's against the store policy to disclose the information for employees at Hay-Way Market. The man finally states. "Madame, I'm sorry, but I will not be able to assist you with that kind of private data."

As Kali stands appealing to the man's weak side, she recalls Glen's closest friend Jameson Milo at SeaShore's Steak and Seafood. Kali apologetically glares over in the gentleman's face hoping he could understand how sorry she was to have troubled him. She's a little embarrassed to have acted so crazy before the man as she makes one last appeal of him to get in touch with Glen. "Sir, if you see Glen would you please let him know Kali Mathias is looking for him. And, she needs to see him right away."

The man smiles somewhat as he assures Kali stating. "I will be sure to give Mr. Monroe your message."

Chapter Nineteen

$\mathcal{L}$eaving Hay-Way Market, Kali felt more abandoned than ever in her core. How could the one man, who she believed would stick around do this to her? She exhales. "How could my heart be so wrong about Glen?"

Sadly walking back to her car Kali decides to call the search for Glen off. Why would Kali be so foolish as to look for a man that doesn't want to be found by her?

Opening the car door, Kali's cell phone starts to ring as she quickly reaches inside the car taking her cell from the seat. Kali notices it was an unfamiliar number as she promptly begins to pray the caller was Glen. Kali thinks by now Glen has lastly come to his senses, and ready to quit playing hide-and-seek with her. Because she's quite tired of a pursuit that's getting her no closer to Glen.

Kali's hand swipes the control on her phone wishing it was Glen. Even though she's somewhat fed up, Kali's heart craves for Glen so right now. She tries to put on a happy tone, uttering. "Hello, this is Kali Mathias!"

In response, the voice Kali had expected to hear was not Glen's. Instead, it's the speech of Jameson Milo, his friend, coldly asserting. "Hello Kali, this is Jameson!"

After Jameson's brief starter, he hesitates for a short spell. He was finding it hard to grasp the fact Kali's that woman who was sending his friend, Glen over the edge this morning. It just does not seem remotely imaginable for Jameson that any woman, much less Kali could ever captivate Glen's heart like she has. But, somehow Kali's magic spell has been cast on Glen; she had his heart.

Jameson couldn't understand why, yet his buddy was head-over-heels in love with Kali. Jameson gently clears his mind as he hears Kali unhappily asks. "Do you have any idea where Glen is? Is he there with you?"

Jameson loosen the air bubble blocking his throat as he inquires. "Kali, I need to see you right away! Are you at home?"

Kali rejoins. "No, I'm in the parking lot at Hay-Way Market where Glen works. Jameson, is Glen alright?"

Ignoring her question about Glen, Jameson stresses. "Wait right there because I am on my way to give you a letter that Glen wanted you to read in his absence!"

Kali's heart is sprinting. She did not understand why Glen was sending Jameson to deliver a letter. Was Glen hurt making it impossible for him to bring her letter for himself. Kali's mind was in a tale-spin with so many not answered questions of what was wrong with her Glen.

In less than ten minutes Jameson's car was pulling in the parking lot of Hay-Way Market. He calls Kali to get her location. Jameson drives around the corner, parking next to Kali's car. He leaps out looking directly into her eyes. "How could you hurt my buddy like that?"

Kali could not comprehend the nonsense Jameson's

lips were babbling about. Specially, when she had called Glen's phone until her fingers were numb and searched the only place she knew to look. Nonetheless, her heart still remains empty of Glen's love or him. So, the words soaring off Jameson's tongue were beyond any requests her lips cared to reply to. Since Kali recognizes the hurt Jameson was speaking about came from the instigations of his friend Martha's tongue.

Kali wasn't definite how to answer Jameson's absurd blames he speaks of as she conveys. "Jameson, what are you trying to infer! Me, hurting Glen because according to your friend Martha, Glen was the wrongdoer here."

Just hearing Martha's name in Kali's sentence. Right then, Jameson starts to shake his head with concern for Glen. Because he recognizes if Martha was mixed-up in anything relating to Glen, this outcome was going to be a catastrophe in the making. However, given these, new crumbs of facts Jameson's listening to about Martha, he couldn't call to mind Glen mentioning her name during their tête-à-tête. Even though, Glen was very distraught overseeing the one woman who he truly loved wrapped in the arms of another man. All Jameson could honestly remember Glen stating over-and-over to him was. How could Kali do this to him when she was suppose to love him so? Jameson had never seen Glen this torn-up over any lady or thing before today.

Jameson's heart pains for Glen. How could Jameson not agree to hand deliver into Kali's hands a letter from Glen? After all, it was Glen's final words of love among him and Kali coming to a conclusion.

Jameson had insisted Glen delivered his note of love to Kali. But, Jameson realizes Glen couldn't bear giving it to Kali face-to-face. Jameson knows if Glen sees Kali, for just a brief moment and smelling the sweet perfume of her skin it will literally break Glen's heart in pieces all over again. Jameson's afraid, Kali's cheating will destroy the new man, Glen, was trying to become for her. Also, Kali's drivel could relapse Glen back to his old lifestyle; the seasonal man. Jameson was certain his friend, Glen, was reliant on all Kali's strength and love behind him to break his cycle. Jameson quickly understands Glen's life minus Kali in it was like Glen being tossed out all alone into such a cruel world without a safety net for survival. Mainly, Kali was Glen's net! Even though, Jameson felt what kind of life either Glen or Kali would live together starting out with deceitful lies; love or not love.

Jameson had warned Glen. Although Glen's essence will suffer a lifetime of unhappiness not being with Kali Mathias, he must let her go. Glen was unwillingly giving back Kali's heart to her. A heart fully detached from his was that right thing to do, Jameson was right. Glen had to give up on a love he would never come by again, and the loss was tearing his heart apart. Jameson could view the anguish within Glen's eyes while handing him Kali's letter and swiftly walking away without another word.

Giving Glen didn't know if he was coming or going. The fact he not once mentioned Martha's name seemed understandable. Yet, Jameson realized when his gullible eyes gazed upon Martha's face, his tender heart will live to regret ever getting back into bed with her. Especially, against his best and only friend, Glen. Because what his soul loathed the most is being a pawn in Martha's chest game where she matches him against Glen. This foolish game, Martha played which seems to always hurt Glen's mate; an innocent victim of Martha's rival with Glen. A game which Jameson hated getting involved and he was starting to regret he ever let Glen talk him into helping.

So jumbled, Jameson says Kali. "So, enlighten me, I wasn't aware Martha was at your house this morning."

Kali breathes heavily, stating. "Martha was not at my house this morning."

"Whew!" Jameson sighs. "Well this answer clears up one thing; it lets me know Martha was not involved."

Kali's puzzled herself now, she asks. "Jameson, have you spoken to Glen or Martha? Because it was Martha's lies about Glen having a girlfriend that started this mess in the first place."

Jameson slightly laughs, saying. "Kali, you've got the wrong idea of why Glen ran. Because it all started when Glen eyes witnessed you in the arms of another man."

"Arms of another man?" Kali inhales slowly because she had no idea what Jameson was talking about.

Jameson promptly returns. "Yes, Glen observed you roughly about seven this morning. You were swathed in the arms of a man on your front steps in night clothes."

"Oh, my!" Kali starts to laugh with relief soon as she realizes it was only Joseph that Glen seen hugging her.

Jameson swiftly retorts. "I actually don't see the joke or humorous side of this; not at all. I truly do not know how you could find it hilarious either. Since Glen's core is shattered, and all because of you, Kali!"

"Oh, Jameson!" Kali joyfully asks. "Where is Glen?"

Jameson rejoinders. "I truly don't know. He gave me the message for you and then he sadly walked away."

Kali expresses with urgency. "If either of us can find Glen then I can straighten out this misunderstanding."

Jameson, still not understanding becomes a bit short with Kali. "Misunderstanding! The way I am seeing this portrayal, Glen busted you red-handed with both hands in someone's cookie jar."

Kali grins, uttering. "I assure you, Jameson, it wasn't like that at all. This is why I need to find Glen!"

Jameson softly laughs. "Kali, if you can persuade any man, let alone Glen, to believe something other than an image his own eyes saw. Then maybe you're a far better woman than I first gave you credit."

Kali knows once the mess was cleared up with Glen, that her and Jameson would definitely revisit that topic.

Right now, Kali's primary focus was on finding Glen and helping him see his way back into her heart. And, if it takes every ounce of the spirit Kali has, she was going to resolve these senseless issues that were keeping Glen away. An unresolved request that was unraveling within both Kali and Glen's core for answers were murking up the sanity of the air between them. It was preventing all their happy tomorrows from coming true or the forever which was now slightly just beyond their existence.

However, just the belief in her heart of seeing Glen's face one more time again was making her heart begin to fall in love with Glen all over. Just that mere thought of Glen's burning passions for her was making Kali's body parts itch for him with such a desire. Kali recognizes he did not have a clue how much her essence was yearning for him. How could Glen know of her sweltering desire for the man who had always spellbound her soul, but at that moment, he was stealing her joy away?

Kali stands before Jameson struggling to hold back a tear from falling. Right now, all she's praying for was to be embraced inside Glen's loving arms. The arms Kali's body was suddenly having such a hunger to be wrapped within as a reminder of Glen's love for her. Kali desires the love and closeness of his body along with the touch of his tender lips. Kali wanted to feel Glen's mouth rest on her lips in a sweet kiss as he steals her breath away.

Kali's sure in her heart that Glen did not realize how lost she was without him. Because if so, there is no way, Glen would have left Kali without leaving a part of him behind with her. Since Glen went away with her craving the scent of his body's entrancing aroma of his cologne, as she softly whispers. "There's just no way Glen would have left me desiring him with only those few words on a sheet of paper encompassing his unfading love for me if he knew." Kali deeply sighs with an air of melancholy as she voices. "There's just no way he would have left!"

Despite the fact, her heart is feeling lost without him being found. Kali was saddened with Glen's decision he made. Even though, the situation with her and Joseph's good-bye rendezvous looked worse than it actually was. Why was Glen not a trusting man? Kali feels twinges of anger setting within her essence as she gazes at Jameson calmly asking. "Why did Glen run away? Why wasn't he more confident in our love or a stronger man?"

Jameson felt her love for Glen even though this hurt shields Kali's face as she glumly stands before him. But, Jameson had no answers that would satisfy this anguish Kali was suddenly sensing for Glen. Jameson shrugs his shoulders replying. "That is a question only Glen would be able to answer for himself; I'm just his best friend."

Just thinking about this nonsense, Kali smiles within as she whispers. "How could Glen ever believe I would ever cheat on a love like ours. Such a foolish man!"

Jameson quickly replies. "Kali, you will have to wear his shoes a little while to realize those answers. All I can tell you right now is Glen's not a perfect man, yet he's a good man."

"Jameson!" Kali heavily exhales asking. "Is there any truth to Martha's lies about Glen's girlfriend?"

Jameson quickly snaps back. "Regardless of anything Martha fills your ears with about Glen, he is still a good man. However; Kali, you must let your heart be the one to answer that question, not me or Martha." He slightly smiles. "But, please take Martha's tales with the grain of salt it's meant to be heard."

Kali shakes her head in agreement with Jameson and smile. Because no matter how much stock she placed in Jameson or Martha's words, the truth was Kali required Glen's passion to breathe. Since Glen was the one man, who truly loved her. Granted, it was not the deep down can't live without you kind of feelings at first, but at the end, Kali's body and soul was tingling for more.

Kali realized that moment Glen came into her lonely

life, he liberated her from a secluded time of heartaches in the making. And, their first date showered Kali's soul with a satisfying warmth which intensified her existence with such an affectionate love. Kali will never let such a love go, she glares into Jameson's face pleading. "If you help me find Glen, I'll make believers out of you both." Kali cogently stares in Jameson's disbelieving eyes as he says. "Kali, I must know the tactics before involving my buddy, Glen, since his heart is already in a fragile state."

Kali realizes once Glen hears all about her earlier era with Joseph, he would totally understand, as she asserts. "Jameson; if you would find him for me, I will show his mistaken eyes how wrong they were this morning."

Jameson confusingly asks. "Do you care to explain?"

Kali recognizes time was wasting away, as she stands before Jameson trying to make the wrong man believe a word of truth.

Chapter Twenty

Kali recognizes Jameson isn't going to lift a finger to assist her. Particularly not without some type of oath to safeguard Glen's core from her. So, after her drawnout exhaling, Kali tries to put Jameson's mind at ease as she appeals. "Right now; Jameson, I actually desire that you trust in my love for Glen. Can you?"

Jameson somewhat laughs as he gazes skyward. "It's a bit difficult to trust you when Glen's heart is suffering because of you. So no; not without more, Kali!"

As Jameson's eyes floats down, Kali catches onto his unsure gaze as she asserts. "I am going to help Glen see the image he witnessed wasn't anything; in the least, like what his eyes believed they perceived to be true."

Jameson glares in her convincing eyes, affirming. "If you're sure you really care for Glen as he do you, then I will help you. But, I truly don't know where he is!"

Kali quickly voices. "Jameson, as his best friend, you must know other people who knows Glen."

Jameson hastily states, "Well, I might know a couple of places I could check for him."

Happily smiling, Kali utters, "Jameson, you go check wherever you need to. Just please bring Glen back!"

As Jameson said goodbye to Kali, he speedily sprints off to go make a few calls to the places where Glen was most likely to be. With Jameson gone to tackle his plan, Kali opens her car door sitting inside. Kali lingers a few more seconds to gather her thoughts before reading the words in Glen's letter. Kali reread each line. She notices it was short, sweet and to the point. Glen wanted her to understand that he loves her more than life itself, yet he must take a little time away from her to think.

As Kali begins to refold Glen's letter and return it to its envelope, several droplets of water streams down on her cheeks. Kali tries so hard to hold back her waterfall. A joyful flow which continues to flow down her face as she blissfully smiles saying. "Oh, Glen if you only knew just how much you are craved within my heart then you would hurry home." Kali's so elated to read in his letter just how much Glen truly did love her.

WHERE WAS GLEN MONROE?

Mourning every second of deserting the best woman he had ever loved. Glen unlocks a door to their family's Georgetown Estate in Washington, DC.

Every iota of vitality drains from his limp body as he walks over this threshold into a lovely pastel floral color hallway. Glen's mind was dog-tired from that vacillating emotion tearing him apart inside of missing Kali.

However; before last night, Kali never was a thought in Glen's life or within his heart. Nonetheless, now Kali or the mention of her name appears to be that regulator for every step he makes. For Glen, she was the tick that causes his core to chime like a clock at noontime by the sweet tone of her voice.

Right then, besides God, Kali had somehow become the pillar of his soul, love of his life! She was the air that he was struggling to breathe; his heart. She was this one woman who had become his everything; his treasures in a lonely world. That only woman, Glen's heart suddenly was pining away for this second as he begins pondering to himself. *Now, why couldn't I be that important in her life as she was in mine? How could I be so wrong about her love for me?*

That moment for Glen seems so final without Kali's touch. Even though in Glen's heart, he prays to gaze on her beauty one last time. But, in Glen's spirit, it appears so unlikely because otherwise why in his heart did it feel he'd just lost his best friend?

Glen, snapping back to reality, he quickly scrutinizes the hallway in search of Jennifer Monroe, his sister, and mother figure. Since Jennifer was the person, who took care of Glen when a tragic car accident stripped both of their parents away when Glen was seven years of age.

Glen, now eyeing his sister Jennifer sitting by herself in a large chair which appears to engulf her whole body. Jennifer's quietly seated by an oversized picture window reading. Glen stands a moment to look, then ducks into the nearest room. A stylishly proportioned dining room dimly lit by such a stunning crystal and gold chandelier.

Glen needed to go unseen for now. He was thirsting for a second alone to toy with the joyful smile on Kali's face. A smile Kali wore while avidly nuzzled in the arms of another man. A painful scene of the man holding his Kali the way only Glen felt he had a right too was more than his core could stand. However, his mind just keeps flashing this scene over-and-over before Glen's weaken eyes. And, every time these pictures reemerge within his head, Glen's heart breaks a little bit more-and-more.

Glen was devastated to recognize the one woman he ultimately gave his heart and soul was unfaithful to him. Even worst, he felt Kali had disrespected everything his love should have meant to them both as Glen whispers. "And, for what, the desires for another man than me!"

Right then, Glen was not ready to face or receive his sister's polite greetings, hugs, or kisses when he had just skipped out on Kali. Glen's heart is still traumatized for choosing to hide himself away like some weakling other than willingly face-up to what was before his eyes. Even if, Glen's soul did only learn to trust Kali in one night.

Glen realizes Kali's betrayal was wrong, but how can he do such a low-down thing to her? How could he run away from Kali? The one-woman his core recognizes as the one love of Glen's life and one that's irreplaceable.

Glen's brain sorts for a way to turn his core off. Yet, how does a man stop his heart from beating for the one woman's heart it's suddenly yoked with? How would he stay away from this woman he was so in love with?

Glen's heart had never ever skipped a beat before; in his life, not for a woman! It wasn't until Glen's eyes rest upon Kali's exquisite inner beauty did his soul truthfully recognize the prettiness she beholds inside and out.

Once such a homely woman in Glen's eyes. Kali had

suddenly gone from the ugly duckling to such a graceful swan in Glen's core during one starry night of ecstasy.

In his heart, Glen prays that walking away from Kali so abruptly; as he had, wasn't going to cost him one last glimpse of her beauty. If so, he would suffer a life of so many regrets. Since he doesn't believe his essence could withstand yearning away for her day-after-day without a last glance.

Unexpectedly, thoughts of never being able to touch Kali's face or to hold her in his arms again is frustrating to Glen. His core starts to ache for her. Glen exhales so vociferously as he tries to wipe away the vision of Kali's arms about another man. So ear-piercing, he didn't hear his sister enter the room. As Glen's sister smartly places her arms about his broad shoulders declaring. "Brother, when did you arrive? I didn't even know you were here. I asked for brunch to be held until you arrived."

Looking at his sister, Glen unhappily says. "Jennifer, I was looking for a few seconds by myself before facing you with all your ebullient hugs and kisses."

Letting go of Glen's neck, his sister stares into those buried sorrowful eyes, "Baby brother, are you okay? Or then again, from the look on your face, who is she?" As Jennifer gives Glen a big hug and kisses on his forehead before lightly laughing at him.

Glen stands up as he towers over his sister. He gives her a bear hug, yet long and soft adorable kisses all over her cheeks, confirming. "Jennifer, you know me so well but let's not discuss it right now." He softly grins saying to his sister. "Today is supposed to be our catch-up day visit. Not a time for dealing with my crazy love issues!"

Glen did not know missing Kali was that transparent to his visage. Glen fingers his hand through his hair and displays a big smile on his face while staring at Jennifer.

Looking into Glen's eyes, his sister avows, "If you're having a problem then so am I, and we can talk about it whenever you are ready!"

Glen, trying to take the focus off his pining away for Kali. He lays his hands upon Jennifer's shoulders asking his sister. "Can we finally go eat brunch now since I am starving, and I know the cook made my favorites?"

Jennifer flashes a pleasant smile at her brother as she slips an arm about his waist. With a little sisterly teasing, they both laugh while strolling away toward this elegant high ceiling formal dining room for brunch.

Close to the dining area, Jennifer takes her arm from around his waistline as she affectionately kisses Glen on his cheek. Leering into her brother's unhappy brownish eyes, she inquires. "Did you even go visit Rehana to tell her you were here because you know you're her pet?"

Rehana Hudson was the family's long-time cook and friend. Rehana had been the cook for this family before either Jennifer or Glen was born. Though Rehana loved them both, Glen was her favorite. And, Jennifer is okay with this because her baby brother was the apple of her eye, too.

Glen looks at his sister smiling as he affirms, "That's because I have all the charm in this family."

Jennifer smiles, expressing. "Well, little brother since you are the charmer. Then go see if you can hurry along Rehana with brunch because suddenly I am starving."

Glen jokingly says, "Jennifer, just watch the charmer in action!" He playfully winks at her blowing a kiss.

Glen continues to joke as he saunters off in the path of the kitchen to see Rehana. Stridently, he rambles into the kitchen area to make his presence known. Hurriedly Rehana's eyes look up to see what all that commotion is in her kitchen. Eyeing Glen, she springs up from where she was sitting and strides over hugging him.

Ecstatically smiling, Rehana takes a step back, as she gives Glen this once overview. Then she proudly utters. "You're such a handsome sight for my old eyes to see!" She walks within inches of Glen as she eyes him up and down before asking. "Why don't you visit us a bit more often? Because I know your sister misses you and so do I. You know we both enjoy fussing over you?"

He returns her enthusiasm, jokingly saying. "Rehana, if you and Jennifer had it your way, I might still be right here with the two of you fussing over me."

Rehana looks at Glen jokingly saying, "And, pray tell me what's so wrong with that?"

Glen laughs affirming. "But, you both do know I am a grown man now and capable of taking care of me!"

She didn't want to hear all his fast-talking because to Rehana, Glen would always be her little boy as she asks. "How's life treating you in the big city grown man?"

Glen smiles answering. "I am quite well, but enough about me, how are you? Because you look fabulous!"

Rehana smartly smiles, stating. "Get out of here, you have always been my little charmer from a small boy."

Glen playfully grins, "You know you are still my girl,

and I realize home is where to visit when I need fussing over."

Rehana leers at Glen as he stands smiling at her with such blameless eyes buried in a youthful face. However, his expression was trying to conciliate what seemed like a world of hurt inside to her.

Glen could plainly see by the way Rehana was eyeing him, she knew his real reason for this visit. Glen tries to laugh it off by kissing her cheek stating. "You're still my favorite girl, but don't tell Jennifer!" He laughs loudly!

Rehana teasingly swats in Glen's path, saying. "Now go ahead, get on out of my kitchen and find Jennifer!"

Glen lingers a second as he plants another one of his sloppy kisses on Rehana's left cheek while laughing. She grins uncontrollably while somewhat lifting her voice to a higher tone exclaiming to him. "Now, will you go and get Jennifer because your brunch is ready to be served." She points her finger in Glen's direction waving it as he exits the kitchen amusingly chuckling.

Leaving the kitchen area, Glen strides into the foyer, where he sees Jennifer on the phone. She was into such an in-depth exchange of words. Jennifer's hands appear to wave in mid-air to a musical tone of her voice. She is chatting and smiling like someone who just won a mega lottery or something close to it. Jennifer's so engaged in conversation, she doesn't hear Glen come back into the hall. Glen wandering nearer to Jennifer, his ears perk up to eavesdrop on her conversation affirming. "Whose so important on the phone, you dare to snub me!"

Hearing Glen, she waves her right hand shooing him

away. Then somewhat upset, she playfully snaps at him. "Go away and mind your own business!"

Jennifer was trying to safeguard Glen and Jameson's years of friendship by not revealing her caller. Since she understands her brother, Glen's a very private man, and he will be annoyed with Jameson. Especially for making public such a heartbreaking part of his life with Jennifer over a phone. Jennifer knew Glen well enough to know he could renounce his friendship with Jameson forever. Mostly, when Jameson was going behind Glen's back to discuss tender issue of Kali's betrayal of Glen. A matter told in confidence that Jameson had no rights revealing to Jennifer. Also, something so distressing for Glen, he never intended to share with Jennifer or anyone besides Jameson and Kali. Even so, Jennifer realized she wasn't getting rid of Glen so fast when his ears were waiting to hear whose robbing her attention from him today.

Chapter Twenty-one

$\mathcal{L}$eering into Glen's eyes, Jennifer shoots a dirty gaze into her brother's path. Glen devilishly continues to nag at her. Becoming a bit fed-up, Jennifer presses her ear a slight more in-depth into the earpiece as she somewhat hastier requests. "Glen, what part of I am on the phone don't you understand? So, go away little brother!"

Hearing Jennifer's stern words, Glen knows she was trying to hide something from him. So, instead of going away, Glen chooses to dillydally a minute. Glen feels he deserves to; at least, overhear Jennifer's side of the little tête-à-tête which she is so adamant on keeping from his ears.

Glen moves in a bit closer to Jennifer. He sights this hollowness over shadow Jennifer's once smiling face. A detached sort of stare which Glen's mind couldn't seem to shake off. Jennifer's eyes glare up into mid-air. Then, after a moment, Jennifer becomes speechless. Even her cocky, but playful attitude seems to dissipate after a few seconds. It was something about those unheard phrases coming through the line which made Jennifer's ears pay closer attention to every spoken syllable. While Jennifer listens, her eyes begin to grow rounder and rounder.

She suddenly appears to glance into Glen's face with

such ardency. Jennifer's heart is aching with distress for her brother as she stands wordless while listening to the heartfelt story shared by Jameson about Glen's Kali.

Glen stands before Jennifer trying to understand her facial expression, but he's stumped. Though, he realizes whoever his sister was speaking with, the individual was indisputably horrifying Jennifer with quite a nail-biter.

Glen unceasingly gaze into Jennifer's stunned face as his eyes spot a swarm of worry wrinkles slowly forming on her forehead. Swiftly, her eyebrows seems to pucker up to join into the groove as Jeniffer's eyes glare toward Glen. She stands ogling at him while shaking her head.

From the strange, but funny gaze on his sister's face, Glen becomes a bit more curious about what the nature of the call could be. Even though Glen believes his ears overheard the mention of Jameson's name as he walked into the area with Jennifer. Nonetheless, the more Glen tries to unravel who Jennifer's speaking to, she conceals the phone with her hands so he wouldn't hear. As Glen suddenly get a little annoyed with his sister, she starts to break her extended period of stillness.

Jennifer restarts her end of the conversation as Glen listens carefully to something that almost sounded like a chuckle. Then while staring in his face, Jennifer releases a hefty sigh before averring. "Now, I really thought you were calling to tell me he squandered away our rights to the Virginia Hay-Way Market's chain of stores."

Hearing those words, Glen's even more confused, as his sister slightly laugh, acclaiming. "For the record, you do know Glen was raised better than that. However, he and I will definitely have a few words once I hang up."

Hearing this scolding sound oozing out of Jennifer's mouth, Glen realizes that couldn't be anyone he knows. Particularly, if he or she was actually expecting his sister to reprimand him as he whispers. "They must be out of their mind wanting my sister to scold a grown man."

Nevertheless, from what his ears were receiving loud and clear someone had an issue with him. And, it seems like the unknown caller was taler-telling on Glen similar to some first grader whose lunch went missing ages ago from one of his pranks. However, this finally made him believe he was wrong to accuse his best friend, Jameson of being the person ratting him out to his sister.

There was just no way that can be Jameson. Because in Glen's topsy-turvy head, he couldn't imagine his best friend, Jameson calling Jennifer to tattle-tale on him. To even think such a thing is utterly absurd for Glen. Then abruptly, Glen distinctly hears flowing off Jennifer's lips the name of his best friend. Glen sharply screeches into her ear. "What ....! Please tell me that's not Jameson on the phone; not my best friend!"

Jennifer frowns at Glen asserting. "Oh, it's Jameson, and don't go anywhere cause we really need to talk!"

Glen's mortified as he stands gawking into Jennifer's face. His tongue dangles in the roof of his mouth as she seems to keep repeating Jameson's name over-and-over in Glen's head until finally, Jennifer ends the call saying. "Jameson, it has been ages since we've spoken and even longer since we've seen one other. So, please visit soon, as I would love to see you." She breathes softly, stating. "And, thanks for letting me know about this chaos that Glen has gotten himself mixed-up into."

As Glen sees Jennifer slowly laying the receiver back on its base, his whole world appears to begin crumbling before his eyes. Glen's having a tough time catching his breath as he gently intones. "Why would a friend betray me like this?" He standstills for a few moments to think it all over. *What will Jameson stand to gain; certainly not Kali? Maybe, Kali has finally convinced Jameson to take her side in her games of betrayal. None of it made sense; not when the two people who pretends to love me are stabbing me in the back. Still, I want to know why Jameson would want to hurt me by teaming up with a woman he doesn't even know; nor did he through Martha?*

With all this disloyalty, Glen realizes why his brain is unsettled. How will he face Jameson or Kali when they both are lying to him? Glen's senses were telling him to turn around and do what he does best; run away. Glen's head was telling him to go as far away as possible rather than face life or be in the same room as Jennifer. If not, Glen will have to admit to this awful shame before him.

He turns to sneak away when Glen sees peeved tears swelling at the edge of Jennifer's eyes. Glen strides over and hug Jennifer lovingly while inquiring. "So, what did Jameson need to speak with you so long about, sister?"

Glen was so afraid that Jameson had disclosed a past that he no longer desires since Kali. Nonetheless, it was one which could rip his sister's heart to pieces if known by Jennifer. And, how could Jameson share his past as a Seasonal Man with Jennifer; no less, over a phone when she's like a sister to him, too. Why would Jameson want to hurt him or Jennifer? The million dollar answer Glen needed to figure out since his essence couldn't bear that weight of suffering too many more pains in his life. Not now, when his heart was still so raw from mourning the lost of Kali's love. Suddenly; without warning, this ache appears to penetrate all throughout his throbbing body.

Glen's tender memories were seizing hold of his raw emotions of his past as the tears starts to flow down his cheek. Glen's so embarrassed for his sister to see such a weak side of him as it exposed a lesser man to her.

Jennifer stands in her brother's arms while her entire being aches for Glen. Jennifer was so helpless while she observes her baby brother's life undergoing such a state of turmoil. However; she recognizes this love thing was so foreign to both her and Glen's essence. Yet, it is that emotional side of Glen's heart, she never wanted to feel as Jennifer fearfully asks. "Baby brother, how can I help you with the agony while putting all judgment aside?"

Jennifer always tried to act as Glen's mother yet now she was grieving for their mother's love to help her out. Mainly now, because Glen's wounded heart required so much more than her little unqualified motherly wisdom has to offer him. Nonetheless, she understands this was one of those times, where Jennifer must think more like a mother; not Glen's sister. Jennifer loosen his embrace while stepping back shaking off her judging feeling. She grabs Glen's cheeks kissing them before cuddling him.

Unleashing that tight hold on Glen, she finds his ear as Jennifer tenderly asks. "Why didn't you tell me?" Just that pleading tone of her voice appears to carve a phase of time out that just stopped. It was as if Glen's life had become immobile from Jennifer's facial expression that seems to have ended all her belief in him.

Glen knows he would have to spill his guts now, but then she squeezes him even tighter saying. "Why didn't I see the hurt inside your eyes, Mother would have?"

Glen returns Jennifer's hug, as he promptly inquires. "What hurt, sister?"

Jennifer raises her hands up to his somewhat chaotic looking face and cuddles it. She glances into Glen's eyes softly affirming. "Jameson told me about Kali, and I am so sorry you are suffering this way. However; according to Jameson, you did what you do best. Glen, you always run away before getting all the facts."

Glen's a bit relieved to know Jameson did not betray his trust; however, upset by what his sister was accusing him of. Glen commences to defend his case. He asserts to his sister. "As my eyes witnessed this neither you nor Jameson was there this morning. So, you didn't see Kali happily swathed up in the man's arms." Glen pauses for a second. Glen needs to purge these reoccurring images of Kali's contentment on her face while held by another man. Disturbed by his own memories, Glen's face turns downhill to prohibit his sister from seeing the wounded soul within. Quickly discovering his voice again, he asks Jennifer. "So what facts do you feel I'm missing here?"

Glen did not want to argue with Jennifer. Especially, about what his eyes might or might not have witnessed. Mainly, since his wounds were still quite raw. He knows that his poor bleeding heart had suffered enough in just one day to last him for a lifetime as his sister glares into his face asking. "How do you know it's love that you're feeling for this woman?"

Glen tenderly replies. "My heart just knows, sister!"

Even if, Glen couldn't explain the intricate workings of his heart, he knew it was love. Because his time away from Kali's love was already feeling much like a hostage take over of the soul. Kali was not there yet her passion was still so spellbinding to Glen's essence.

Nevertheless, it was not the time for a pity party; not for him. Mainly, Glen came home for this short-term to refuel himself with a little of Rehana's southern cooking and Jennifer's nourishing. A quick fixer which Glen had not been able to do since arriving. He stares at Jennifer, uttering. "Rehana is ready to serve brunch, and we both know she'll be upset if it gets cold. So, let's go eat while it's still hot because I am suddenly starving!"

Jennifer was famished, yet she wanted to understand the love her brother was speaking of and why he was so willing to let it go. She fervidly asks, "Glen, why are you so quick to dismiss the feeling for someone you say you love so dearly?"

Glen hurriedly comes back with sadness in his voice. "Sister, just the mere thought of seeing Kali in the arms of the man continues to tear my heart to shreds. Now if the throbbing pain inside which I feel is not love, please tell me what is?"

"Glen!" Jennifer exhales out. "What you're believing in your heart to be love, just might be a touch of envy."

Glen takes her by the arm as he says. "Sister, let's go sit down and have brunch while I tell you all about it."

As they stroll off toward the dining room, Jennifer is sensing there's so much more to Glen's story with Kali. But whatever it was she would listen, then her and Glen would try to sort out his true feelings for this woman.

Approaching the dining room, Jennifer and Glen see Rehana busy setting up the table for brunch as she asks. "Where have you two been? I sent you for Jennifer, and you both go missing while your brunch is getting cold!"

Glen smiles uttering, "Sorry, it was my hold-up. But, we are here now and both quite hungry."

Rehana says, "Good since I fixed all your favorites."

As Rehana leaves the room, Glen's tongue opens up like a broken water faucet. Glen starts to tell Jennifer all about his big city life as the Seasonal Man and also how he met Kali Mathias at the Hay-Way Market.

Jennifer sits quietly through Glen's heart-wrenching, and distasteful life details. It was as if this bombshell to her gut has severed a hole in her heart as Jennifer heard what Glen's life had become while living in Virginia.

She rests her fork on the side of her plate as Jennifer unexpectedly loses her desire for the delectable treats in front of her. Instead, her taste buds were replaced by an overwhelming guiltiness. It appears like the more words Jennifer's ears heeds from his tongue, a shameful regret rips at her soul for whoever this man is which Glen was speaking of.

As Glen's sister impatiently sits across from him, she is unsure of who he is. Suddenly, she's sensing that part of her being which joins a sister's trust to her brother, it was slowly becoming undone. Jennifer's heart could not bear to listen one second more as she stands up walking around the table near him. She sympathetically stares in Glen's face as her arms reaches out and grab on to him. She hugs him tightly while whispering in his ear. "Glen, please stop because who are you? This man, before me, I no longer recognize him as my baby brother anymore. At least, not the one that you're speaking of."

Glen stops with tears in his eyes. He turns around to face Jennifer as she begs Glen to quit speaking of a past which in her mind is imperceptible to his own sister.

Chapter Twenty-two

Glen grasps from the distress coating Jennifer's face. He sadly moans as Glen recognizes his sister isn't ready to bear all the veracities of his past right now. Yet, Glen knows within his heart, he needs his sister's blessings to find any desire to seek Kali's love ever again.

He woefully pleads with Jennifer for her forgiveness, as Glen leers at Jennifer with weeping eyes begging her. "Sister, can you please forgive me?" He wipes his soggy eyes before carrying on. "Because I never meant to hurt you with my sinful deeds toward women."

As his sister stands before him voiceless with eyes of heated tears, Glen's heart pains for Jennifer as he gently affirms. "Sister, I am not very proud of that man either, but it was the life of your brother before meeting Kali."

Just as Kali's name rolls off his lips, Glen's heart was awaken by a jolt of realism. How could he ever get Kali; the woman he truly loved, to forgive him when his own sister's heart appears to be struggling with forgiveness?

As Glen thinks over his life choices, he unexpectedly overhears an indistinct but somewhat sympathetic tone. Jennifer begins to speak. Her voice appears to be a little stifled by the heartfelt tears streaming down her sadden cheeks. Jennifer raises her hands up surrounding Glen's face. What Jennifer wishes to ask, her eyes want to glare thru that window of Glen's soul to understand. Jennifer requests for something only he and God knew. "Why?"

The sound seem to continually repeat over-and-over inside Glen's soul for a straightforward reply to just one word, he remains quiet. Mostly, because Glen knows by the misery reflected on Jennifer's face, she already knew her own response. Yet, Jennifer desires to let Glen hear himself speaking those ugly words out loud for his core to see his own "why" wasn't what he truly believed it to be all these years. And, only the sound of his own voice Jennifer knows will allow Glen to seek repentance.

In her heart, Jennifer realizes it was Glen's first steps toward the likelihood of recapturing Kali's love back or his own healing. She grasps only through his ears would Glen's heart unmask that actual cause for such behavior toward a woman. Jennifer desires Glen to recognize the action of a seven years old boy, whose missing the arms of a mother's love. Even if, Jennifer realizes what might be the root cause, she still awaits Glen's response. Since Jennifer knew her brother's retaliation couldn't possibly be about any shady greed for a dollar bill.

Disgracefully Glen can only shrug his shoulder as he lowers his head. He hides his eyes from this intensity of a stare he can't bear to see colored with dislike of him.

Glen felt; in his own defense, it all occurred after the humiliating state of being left at the altar. That mockery of a woman justified his exploitations, but what he does not understand is why he choose to blame all women.

Even if, the unforgivable game Glen's heart suffered was indisputably a deal breaker of him ever desiring the love of a woman ever again. Still, the anguish from it all make every fiber within Glen's entire body desire to get even. So for Jennifer, Glen narrates these spoken words aloud to hear. "A wounded heart, I held responsible for all my sinful revenge on women." As the blaming tones discharges off Glen's lips, he suddenly knows it was not a woman's love. Glen understood all of his love glitches goes so much deeper for him. Yet, hearing this problem out loud, it's still unbelievable for Glen's heart to clearly grasp. Mostly, because his very soul was once torn apart by what a woman; he loved so passionately, called love.

It was five years ago to date. The precise day when a tender, loving soul became what was known to many as a Seasonal Man. A moment that changed Glen's trust in the love of a lady when so many crave after him.

Glen's affection for all women was being substituted for his desires for a twisted shade of green. The intrigue for just a small hint of his spurn for avenge on females.

Glen's payback looked-for a woman whose self-love stripped him of his love, money, and respect. A woman has injured Glen's heart, and now all must pay the price of one. Well, that was yesterday's, Glen. The revengeful man who's soul sought after a woman's love as a means of justice for his own colorful existence.

Notably, those ladies, whose losses could harm them

the most became the prong of Glen's love game. That's until Glen's heart encountered Kali's kind of passion.

A desire for Kali's love is the therapy for Glen to get over his broken heart and reopen his eyes to love again. This resuscitated man, Glen will finally allow himself to discern the torment of his licentious conducts wasn't an exotic brand of love. Now gazing in his sister's sad face, Glen sees all the hurt faces caused by his lack of respect traded for lust, betrayal, and revenge.

Jennifer was the one who Glen loved more than any; including Kali. Jennifer was not just his loving sister but the only mother figure growing up. Jennifer was the last person, who Glen ever desired to cause grief. It was too late, Glen can feel Jennifer's pain inside her heart as she stands gazing in air. His own sister didn't recognize that man's voice ripping thru her ears were the same tone as her brother's voice. Also, at that instance, Glen's having a trying time distinguishing it's truly him speaking, too.

Glen regretfully probes for Jennifer's understanding, as he gently breathes, asking. "Jennifer, I thought it was a woman's love which had victimized me so, why?"

Jennifer tries to understand why Glen felt love could have wronged him. And, perhaps why he sort after a bit of eye-for-an-eye type of retaliation, but her core would not. Jennifer's heart couldn't come to terms with any of the reasons love should take the blame for her brother's incivility toward women as she loudly voices. "How did love force you to become so cruel when it's so beautiful to behold. Particularly, when both hearts are joined into this union together, brother?"

Her words shamed Glen as he looks away to avoid a battle of the eyes with his sister. Yet, he could sense her agony as the intensity of Jennifer's words penetrates his soul searching for an answer for what love was to him.

Abruptly, Glen's exploit has Jennifer questioning her own heart as to what love truly meant to her.

Both, Jennifer and Glen found themselves searching their essence for clarity to love as the room goes utterly soundless. For nearly thirty-minutes, both of them were in a state of bewilderment without being any closer to a meaning for love. Then without warning Glen hears the gentle tone of his sister affirming. "Baby brother, if you love Kali, then maybe you still have time to correct that dreadful chaos which your eyes have gotten you into."

Nevertheless, Jennifer knew as the accusatory verses departed her lips it was useless. She already knows Glen was way too obstinate to give into his pigheaded proud. Glen turns toward Jennifer. Glen upsettingly glares into her face as he inquires. "Are you implying my eyes were lying to me this morning?"

Sensing Glen's pride kicking in, she says. "Of course not! Glen, what I'm saying is maybe Kali deserves to be heard before you go dismissing her love altogether."

Gasping a long-drawn-out breath of air, Glen stands up saying. "Me, dismissing Kali's love!" He sucks a little air thru his teeth before going on. "Well; my dear sister, I believe Kali's actions today spoke volumes all on their own."

Jennifer takes Glen by the hands, as she motions for him to sit back down and hear her out. As the verses of Jonah and the Whale 1:1-17, surface to Jennifer's mind. The bible story their mother use to tell her and Glen as kids which makes her quickly realize if God placed Kali in Glen's life to make a difference, he couldn't run away from it. No different than Jonah, he could not run away from Nineveh; at least, not before doing what God had purposed for Jonah's life. Thus; Jennifer prays God has place Kali in her brother's life to make Glen's core love again and repent. Jennifer knew if God could use Jonah to restore the Ninevites by repentance, He can certainly use Kali's love to restore Glen's faith. Jennifer validates, "Brother, God can use what we believe as just common circumstances and turn it into blessings and deliverance for His people as within the story of Jonah. So, brother right now, I have enough faith for us both."

Even with all her faith, Jennifer realizes forcing Glen to accept Jameson's belief of Kali's truth is not going to be easy. In fact, Jennifer recognizes it just might be near impossible without prayer. And, taking a gander at what Jennifer is currently dealing with, she could see it wasn't going to be without a fight with Glen. Not when he still accept as true his lonely heart had been broken again by the love of a woman; Kali's love.

Even more, Jennifer could sense the disrespect Glen felt as he glares at her affirming. "Besides, Kali and that man has saddled my soul with such sadness and hurt. It is a feeling which I'm finding unbearable to shake off."

Of course, Jennifer recognizes this was her brother's self-pride. Or, perhaps his jealousy that wouldn't permit his soul to admit such an awful reality. The fact his eyes might have been mistaken. Glen's destiny with Kali was nesting at the mercy of a pair of untrusting eyes, and his wounded heart masquerading itself as true love.

Love or lust, Jennifer realizes she was fronted with a delicate issue. As she knows it's outcome could be quite essential to Glen's future as a trusting man. And, for no other reason than this, she didn't want to push him into making a decision. Not before thinking it through; even if Jennifer believes Glen's heart needs to hear a word of assurance first. Jennifer knows only Kali's tongue could offer Glen that certainty required which will permit him to experience the beauty of a woman's love ever again.

Jennifer breathes worryingly before calmly inquiring. "Glen, do you think; perchance, it might be possible for you to trust your heart on this one?"

Knowing he still loves Kali, Glen looks at her stating in a delicate voice. "Yes, anything is possible but how is my heart suppose to deal with my pain after the trust?"

Inside his heart, Glen could no longer detect a sense of hope or belief because all he was seeing is betrayal. A feeling which is obscuring his real emotions.

Glen senses he was still very much in-love with Kali. Still, his core was grieving too much to think of desiring her passion as his cell phone begins to ring.

Glaring into Glen's face, Jennifer says. "Glen, please answer your phone." Suddenly standing up, she places a hand on his right shoulder as she gently smiles uttering. "I asked Jameson to have Kali call you."

Glen frowns as he asks. "Sister, how could you?"

Jennifer answers, "Glen, you can't hide here forever. So, speak with Kali and work it out, if you love her."

There wasn't a pulse in Glen's body that doesn't still love Kali, so he answers. "Hello, this is Glen Monroe!"

His soul starts to ache from the sexy sound of Kali's voice as she pleas. "Baby, where are you? I have been in a frenzy searching all over for you!"

Then just as bad as his soul ached, his skin begins to crawl as he coldly ask. "And, why would you be looking for me, Miss Mathias?"

Jennifer senses a bit of pity for Kali as her brother is being aloof with her. So, before Jennifer leaves the area, she looks into Glen eyes uttering. "Please stop being so hostile with your words to Kali, and just hear her out. If not for you, then for me!"

He nods his head as the tone of his voice becomes a little more lenient as he pleads. "Kali, perhaps we could begin over again?" As Glen utters that sentence to Kali, even he didn't know what the words entailed for them.

Kali notices that chill in his tone, but she chooses to ignore it. Mainly, since she was just so thrilled that Glen received her phone call after so many attempts. So, Kali starts again by asking. "Hello Glen, how are you?"

But, even if, Glen's essence desires to begin over, his mind was whispering within. *How could you take Kali back into your life when once a cheater, always a cheater? Yet the softer tone of his sister's voice was in the background cautioning him to; at least, hear Kali out.*

He wants to hear what Kali has to say; however, was he suddenly suppose to forget what he had seen. Glen's head is so topsy-turvy because dissimilar to the woman, whose love he thought was real, Kali's was different.

Although his core ached so, Kali's passion still made him want to do the right thing. Glen clears his throat as he replies. "Other than my heart pains for you, I believe I am well."

Kali's happier than she had been that entire day. She couldn't be sure, yet what her ears are hearing in Glen's tone sounds like he's missing her. Never once did Kali's mind conjure up in the past hours when Glen was gone that she would miss his melodious sound so much. Kali ardently answers. "Oh Glen, it is so good to finally hear the melodic tone of your sweet voice again in my ear!"

In Glen's head, he was thinking this is truly Martha's friend; even phony like her. Nevertheless, Glen chooses to have a few moments of thrills until he flips the script on Kali, confirming. "Kali, I desired to surprise you this morning, so I stopped by your house. I wanted the tone of my voice to be the first tune in your ears." Hastily he stops talking before his speech turns cold in Kali's ear.

Chapter Twenty-three

*K*ali listens to a somewhat unfriendly tenor traveling through the line as her heart appears to melt in its track. Suddenly, Kali's grasping what Glen's letter was stating. And, it sadden her to just realize Glen didn't want to be found; at least, not by her as she regretfully sighs. "Why didn't Glen wish to be seen, if he truly love me?"

Nonetheless, even though Glen didn't wish to speak or see her, Kali realizes the silly little emotionless games of pretend must end. Because Kali's core was shattering a little more with every tongueful of regret she senses in her soul for finding Glen. Right then, she recognizes an innocent play on words were about to get quite ugly for them both regardless of their love for each other.

In particular since what ended in both of their hearts last night appearing like love seem to be sounding more like a sign of discord. Especially, when they both thinks it was the other who wronged them.

Kali and Glen's ears endure reproachful words from each other's lips of blame. All while their essence sink a little more with each word. Their own voices are getting to be more than either of the souls can stand when they looked-for terms of passion to entertain their ears.

Kali and Glen's heart was yearning to hear the sweet musical notes of love their ears had grown accustom to hearing from one another. Because at that very moment Kali and Glen were craving for one another's kisses and sweet caresses. The unquenchable hunger which merely hours ago had them both longing for a forever. A thirst that had Kali and Glen dreaming of a fairytale existence with hopes of so many tomorrows together.

In either of their hearts, it wasn't a doubt how much passion exist. However; their longing to love, it just was not enough to make the insensitive words to each other end. Not unless Glen was willing to accept the blame of a soul that's too bitter to realize it might be wrong. Kali knows one of them must be willing and clearly, she sees Glen isn't. She speaks up to admit her role in their mess up. Mainly, since it was her hugging Joseph that initially caused the image for Glen's false sight to witness.

Kali swiftly scrutinizes her own soul while entreating God in prayer. Kali starts to pray for a change in Glen's way of thinking. "Lord, please alter a foolish man's eyes to see that same vision of the truth which only You and I know to be real?" As her prayer ended, Kali continues to rake thru her head before voicing. "Jameson gave me your letter. Yet, after reading it, I felt you wanted me to find you!" Kali softly laughs, "However, after exploring my soul and seeking God, now my answer is clearer."

Glen sharply asks. "And, what did you discover?"

Kali somewhat laughs, declaring. "Glen, I do believe

your fading eyesight along with such a foolish pride was more than enough love for you without me around."

Sensing a touch of lost, Glen fervently replies, "Kali, I am sorry if my actions resulted into such nonsense for you to believe. As my entire soul has been solely owned by you, Kali, from the instant, I seen you open the door dressed in red."

"Then why did you shut me out?" Kali implores him for an answer. "And, what was I suppose to think when you left, without even a good-bye, after leading my core on with all your unfilled promises for today?"

Heavily breathing, Glen replies, "Kali, that song "At Last" and our passionate kiss only sealed the love in my heart for you." Yet, as these lyrics were being expressed to Kali, he still has doubt. In Glen's mind, his ears were still grasping a hint of blame from Kali's tongue toward him. Somehow, each chosen syllable Kali spoke seemed to be spelling out only Glen's faults in her speech. And, lastly, Glen's ears has had enough of Kali's games as he shrieks into the receiver. "Kali, please let's cut this crap! Since it was my sister, Jennifer, and Jameson who asked you to call here; not me." As these words escape Glen's lips, his heart knew it was untrue. Because, for him, just the fact Kali called meant she had not given up on him.

Kali breathes in softly as she asserts. "Yes, let's drop all this playacting with each other. Because if you would have confronted me this morning; instead of running, it would have never come to such unpleasantries."

Glen lightly laughs as he asks. "What kind of fool do you take me for, Kali? What am I suppose to do when I see the woman, I love in such a compromising situation as my eyes seen you in the wee hours of the morning?"

"Honey," Kali ardently expresses. "If you would just resurface, it will be so much easier to work things out."

Without even giving it any thought, Glen spouts off, "Kali, I will be back tomorrow night. However; not to a bunch of lies because my heart can't take it. Not when I am so in-love with you."

In Kali's heart, she senses even another moment was too long for her to wait on Glen to come to his sanity.

Kali realizes it is time to tell her truths whether Glen believes her or not as she begins confessing. "Your eyes couldn't of been more wrong about me. Since this man, which your eyes perceived to witness this dying passion for didn't exist. Although, I do think it is what the devil desired for you to see, and you sanctioned Satan's bait."

Glen sounds a bit unforgiving as he growls, "Kali, in whose mind was this devil you speak of? Because in my perfect vision of your picture, it spoke for itself!" While asking his question, Glen wonders. *Who is fooling who here with a play on words; me or Kali?* As Kali's lyrics forces him to now ponder whether her version of what Glen's eyes had boldly witnessed was of the devil. Deep in thought, Glen's ears overheard Kali emphasizes. "Yes, all in your made-up world for what your kind of love patterns!"

Glen's shocked to even hear her words reference his kind of messed-up love. It was as if Kali's desires of the heart was fast becoming not the same as his passions.

He scrutinizes Kali's mind. "Kali, what has Jameson,

and his sidekick Martha done to cast any distrust on my life, or; better yet, my love for you?"

Kali intensely thinks before she poses a question the ears didn't wish to hear. "It was purely your actions! So, what shocks do Jameson or Martha know that's corrupt enough to taint your love in my eyes?"

Glen cautiously returns her answer since he is aware, he and Kali must talk. Yet, it isn't a conversation taking place over the phone as Kali deserves better. His dialog gradually becomes kinder as Glen tries to avoid any talk about Jameson or Martha until a face-to-face with Kali.

Glen asks. "Devil or not! Kali, why was you hugging the man in your sexy lingerie this morning?"

Kali passionately utters. "Glen, due to the respect of the love I have for you, I didn't invite him inside. Yet, I wanted to say goodbye since Joseph's leaving town."

Glen hears her words leaving town as his soul senses a startling calmness before restating. "Still, why was you hugging Joseph in your sleepwear? Particularly, after the confession of your love for me just hours before?"

She now senses the jealousy in Glen's speech as Kali tenderly discloses her and Joseph's relationship to Glen. She moanfully sighs before uttering. "Joseph and I were once lovers. Well, that was what I believed until Joseph broke my heart in tiny small pieces as he walked out for Carol Benson, the woman next door." As her words are so relatable to Glen's heart, he caringly replies, "I didn't know!" As Glen listens to this distress in Kali's tone, he detects what a butt-head he had been. Also, Glen didn't have a right to accuse Kali of such a wily act. Not when Glen's own past was quite dubious itself. He recognizes nothing in Kali's life could ever be more catastrophic or sinister than his before knowing her love.

Kali tearfully undertones as just the mention of what Joseph had done to her brought back this foul memory. Kali whispers. "How would you have known Glen, as it was you who didn't want to discuss our past?"

Glen listlessly starts to talk. "It wasn't your past Kali that I was afraid to know, it was you knowing mine."

Kali softly utters. "But, I'm not understanding you."

Glen slowly exhales as he voices. "Well, this is going to require a face-to-face. It is one of the reasons, I came by this morning to share my past, present, and future."

In Kali's mind, she instantly jumps to the worst-case scenario. *Was he trying to break-up with me? And, even before giving us the chance at a forever or a tomorrow; the nerve of Glen!* As Kali clears her head of the what if's, Kali softly asks. "Well, what's so wrong with you sharing this news over the phone since I am all ears?"

Glen tenderly replies, "Kali, it's not a subject worthy of your ears hearing over a phone." He hesitates while a long gust of wind escapes his lungs before going on. "It is my past; however, one that can shatter your dreams."

At this point, Kali wasn't sure she even wants words from Glen's lips over the phone or in-person. Since the language was of a dialect, her core didn't care to grasp.

Suddenly, Kali's wishful dreams of being with a man like Glen with a sorted past was becoming a horror film as she softly breathes into the phone saying. "What's so distasteful could your lips reveal which I haven't already heard about you over the years?"

Glen heavily moans before voicing. "Kali, what your ears heard from Martha's gossip. Well, it might have the implication of hatred within for me."

Kali catches her breath then saying. "Glen, I realized our date was purely about a financial gain for you, yet it started as only a fulfillment of lust for me."

Glen cuttingly roars, "Kali, what nonsense! That's so hard for me to believe about the woman I love!" As the lies intruded upon Glen's beliefs of Kali, he demands to know. "Why are you trying to hurt me with these lies?"

Kali softly whispers, "Glen, please let me finish what I am saying. Mostly, what started as a lustful craving for me; so many years ago, last night became much more."

Glen regretfully moans as he states. "Well, this could switch to an emotion of hate once you hear my story."

Kali couldn't envision what Glen will say; so cruel, it will alter her heart's desire for him. When unexpectedly, she overhears a delicate tone whisper. "Well, open your door, if you are ready to hear the truths from my lips!"

As Kali slowly walks to the door, she feels like a love which she fought so hard to make hers was going away. Yet, when Kali opened her door and saw Glen standing there. Kali finally recognized his love was like having an entire world at your feet but losing your soul to keep.

Glen strolls in as he pauses to kiss Kali on her cheek before saying. "I believe you need to be seated for what I have to share with you about my life up until as recent as every breath I took until right here and now."

With Glen just showing up without a warning, Kali's

nerves were on edge. As she directs Glen in the path of the sofa, she softly asks. "Were you outside all along?"

Glen tenderly chuckles as he replies. "No, but I realized both our hearts desire some honesty to sleep tonight."

Kali laughs before asking. "Glen, so all this time you were right here; perhaps with your girlfriend?" As these distrustful words departed her mouth, Kali knew it was only her jealousy speaking.

Glen bothersomely says. "Oh, I see Martha has been talking to you, but I wasn't with Jo-Ann." He smirks. "I was visiting my sister, Jennifer, who lives thirty minutes away in the Georgetown area of Washington D.C.!"

Even though Glen wasn't with the girlfriend, neither did he ever contradict Kali about having one. Kali sadly inquires. "So, you do have a girlfriend?"

Glen quickly affirms. "Yes, Kali, but it's you! Since it was your love, I had been seeking all these years and yet I never realized it before last night."

"Glen!" Kali says as she lowers her head voicing. "If it's me, then what about Jo-Ann Parks; your girlfriend?"

Glen proudly asserts. "Kali, that is why I was at your house so early this morning. I went to see Jo-Ann; since Kali, she's one of the ladies that my past had wronged." Before Glen can finish speaking, Kali interrupts stating. "I am lost, please help me to understand since that love you freely speak of hinges on your truth."

Glen states as he looks away. "Kali, regardless of the stained character of me spoken from my lips, I honestly do love you." As Glen begins his life tales of a Seasonal Man, he reveals a wicked past to Kali of greed, lust, and deceit.

Yet, with Kali, he goes one step further. He talks about the underlining root for his actions. "Please try to understand, I was only seven when my parent's died. So a woman's love meant security for me. It was somehow a connection to a missing mother's love. Yet, the hands of a woman's love; who I adored so, it made a different man of me. She used my heart up, then threw it away."

As the tears starts to run down Glen's face, Kali lifts her hands up, wiping each eye as she kisses him, stating. "Glen, I am so sorry for a past that I can only pray God gives you peace. Yet, what I can offer is a present and a future of timeless love without deception or greed. But, not as your seasonal woman. Somehow as these idioms were spoken, Kali realizes Glen no longer needs to hide behind any image as the Seasonal Man; not when God's love has set them both free to love again. And, together Glen and Kali reclaimed hearts of love and a life of joy.

Glen brushes Kali's face delicately as he passionately states. "Kali, every day of each year isn't enough for me to love you. As in you, I have found a woman's love, so heartfelt; how would my heart desire another?" He leers into Kali's enquiring eyes as he inhales gently, going on. "Kali, I am just a lonely man who sits before you asking you to give our love a second chance … will you?"

About the Author

*E*loise's novels: A Twisted Shade Of Green and Escaping Rapture Of Devotion was written with a message for all women, who society has taught they are less desirable to anyone because of being victimized in any way. The shade of skin, weight, texture/length of hair, level of education, living environment, job status, etc. Well, that list can go on and on. But, through Eloise's writings and speaking engagements, she prays to empower all women not to accept the labels which society has branded us with; instead, the one that God gave His only Son for us to achieve.

Eloise's cause is to empower women through trust and faith in God to know He equipped us with "Choice"! So, women through the novel, she prays to furnish you with the words on all pages to elect their rights to stand-up and be proud of who we are; regardless of what others think! And, even though, our lives may or may not parallel the character in the book, the fairy tale happy ever after. It can be represented by all the struggles she endured and the trust and faith she possessed to achieve her faithful ending. And, just like God, answered her prayers, He will do the same for us. Contact information:

Website: http://www.emackinn01.com

blog: http://www.mackinnonbooksolution.com